ARK OF BLOOD

AN ARKANE THRILLER
J.F. PENN

Ark of Blood. An ARKANE Thriller (Book 3)
Copyright © Joanna Penn (2012, 2015). All rights reserved.
Second Edition. Previously published as EXODUS

www.JFPenn.com

ISBN: 978-1-912105-71-7

Requests to publish work from this book should be sent to:
joanna@CurlUpPress.com

Cover and Interior Design: JD Smith Design

Printed by Lightning Source

CURL UP
PRESS

www.CurlUpPress.com

"Have them make an ark of acacia wood …
overlay it with pure gold …
Then put in the ark the tablets of the covenant
law, which I will give you."

Exodus 25: 10-16

"God struck down some of the men of Beth
Shemesh, putting 70 of them to death because
they had looked into the ark of the Lord.
The people mourned because of the heavy
blow the Lord had dealt them."

1 Samuel 6:19.
Septuagint version and Hebrew manuscripts
report 50,070 killed.

THE DAY
BEFORE

PROLOGUE

Museum of Egyptian Antiquities, Cairo, Egypt. 1.34am

DJINNS SEEP FROM THE cracks of the primeval city as Anubis prowls the Egyptian night in search of the dying. The gods of the ancients are buried deep under Africa's largest city, but in the dark they claw their way back into consciousness, clinging to eternal life through a remaining glimmer of faith.

Youssef Diab concentrated on the final clue of his crossword puzzle, the only noise the hum and whirr of fans that failed to cool the stifling summer heat. He was the only guard on duty tonight because the security company had sent all the men round to the businesses surrounding Tahrir Square. After the political riots of the Arab Spring, they were paying the most for enhanced security so the museum was silent and still, its only occupants the dead.

Suddenly a scream rang out, the noise tinny through the security screen and Youssef was jolted from his crossword, his skin prickling at the haunting sound. It was sharp at first, then trailed off into a trembling moan. Youssef scanned the screens, switching views until he saw movement within the Amarna Period section of the museum.

Knowing there was no one else around to help, Youssef pressed the silent alarm anyway. With some luck, a security team would come and investigate before the intruders left. He squinted at the screen. It looked like they were doing something to the giant statues but he couldn't see properly who or what had screamed so terribly. Pulling his gun from its holster, Youssef headed downstairs. He had to try to stop them, or he would pay with his job.

On the ground floor, he rounded a corner into the Amarna suite of rooms and inched forward with caution, hugging close to the cramped display cases, where giant heads of pharaohs jostled with mummy cases and the detritus of a long-dead civilization. As he moved closer, Youssef heard another sound, an animal moan that cut through him. He hurried towards it, gun drawn but his shoes squeaked and he froze mid-stride, heart pounding. They didn't pay him enough to risk his life so easily. He listened carefully but heard no one approach, so he crept on tiptoe to the doorway and peered between two display cases at the scene before him.

A man was tied, spreadeagled, between two massive sculptures, his arms outstretched to the ancient gods as they stared impassively down at his suffering. His shirt was ripped open and blood dripped down to pool at his feet from the sign carved on his chest. It was an ankh, the key of life formed in the shape of a cross with a looped handle, a symbol of eternal life. The man's face was swollen and bloody from a beating but Youssef realized with a start that the man was one of the specialist curators, Dr Abasi Gamal.

A woman stood in front of him holding a ceremonial knife. A tight black outfit emphasized her feminine curves and a mask of the falcon God Horus covered her face. Around her stood others in the guise of gods made flesh and Youssef recognized Anubis, the jackal and the baboon-headed Thoth. The woman caressed the knife handle as she drew the blade over Abasi's chest again, cutting lines into his flesh as she spoke.

"Where is it Abasi? I know you've studied it for many years and that you've found something new recently. I need to know where the Ark is."

Abasi looked back at her and Youssef could see a curious fanaticism glinting in his eyes.

"You'll never find it," he said. "The Ark has protected itself for generations and it will remain safe from you now. I curse you ..."

"Enough," she shouted, slamming the blunt end of the knife into his solar plexus. He grunted and slumped against his bonds. "I have your journals and I will find your research assistant. I don't need you, but the gods need a sacrifice to bless my quest."

Youssef heard arousal in her voice, the tones of expectancy as she considered her prize. Abasi looked up at her, his eyes terrified, voice trembling.

"No, you cannot. Please, I would be without rest for eternity."

The woman beckoned the figures of Anubis and Thoth forward. The men under the masks had muscled arms that allowed no chance for escape as they unhooked Abasi and dragged him to one of the sarcophagi that littered the museum. The Curator struggled and called out in a language Youssef couldn't understand but it sounded like a plea to the gods to spare him.

"The sarcophagus is appropriate," the woman purred. "For the word means flesh-eater and that is what it shall be for you. This rite is ancient and you should be flattered that your body is to be treated as the Pharaohs were. Of course, they were dead before the process began."

The men tied the Curator onto the lid of the sarcophagus, stuffing a gag into his mouth so that his moans became muted. He struggled frantically but the ropes held fast, cutting into his wrists. Youssef watched in horror as the woman turned and smashed a display case containing the tools of the mummification process, salvaged from one of the tombs in the Valley of the Kings. She selected a chisel and a hammer, caressing the objects, as if anticipating the pleasure to come.

Youssef realized with horror what she was about to do but he was frozen with fear, unable to move. He could only watch as the woman took the thin chisel and hammer and approached the tied man, intoning prayers as the other men responded with a repetitive chorus. Youssef heard the desert in her voice, ancient prayers that called upon gods he had thought long dead. Abasi tried to squirm away, screaming into his gag but Anubis held his head still like a vice in his meaty hands.

Delicately, as if trying not to mark him, the woman inserted the chisel up one of the Curator's nostrils, her voice rising to a final high note. With a light tap, she banged the chisel and blood spurted out around the instrument. Abasi grunted and she tapped again, harder this time and his eyes rolled back in agony.

"You can still stop this, Abasi," the woman said, her voice eerily calm for the bloody scene she was creating. "Tell me where the Ark is, for according to the ritual, you must be disemboweled before I drag your brain from your skull." Abasi moaned against his gag, thrashing his head in a violence of denial. She shook her head. "So be it."

Gently, as if she was just leaning into him as a lover would, she began to press the knife into his left side. It was blunted from millennia of disuse, so it was hard to penetrate his skin, but she persisted, sawing it to and fro to pierce the curator's side. As she pushed the knife in, the woman began to breathe faster and Youssef could sense her excitement at this act of intimate violation. He knew he should run, should find help to save the man, but he was transfixed by the horror as Abasi groaned in tortured agony. The masked figures began chanting again, their voices louder now, in words that animated the primitive horror of this place.

Once the tip of the knife blade was in, the woman started to zigzag it through Abasi's skin, slicing at his flesh. The curator was convulsing, arching away from her but still held down by his bonds and the deities surrounding him. Blood gushed over her hands as she continued cutting, opening up his side. She didn't flinch, just drove the knife deeper until the cut was long enough, then she reached into Abasi's body and pulled out a loop of his intestines, the stink of it making one of the men gag. Blood and bodily fluids pumped in gouts onto the floor but the curator was still squirming. Youssef gasped, realizing that the man wasn't dead yet, and the woman wasn't finished.

"Men have watched their intestines burned before them before they died," she said, "but for you, we will finish in the traditional way."

She reached for the long chisel. This time she slammed it up his nose and smashed the hammer into it once, then twice. At the second blow, the chisel emerged from the top of his skull, brain matter and bloody skull fragments dripping from it. The curator gave a loud cry, shuddering as his body arched one more time, before he lay still. The woman calmed her breath as she looked down on the corpse, her clothes stained with his blood, his guts steaming on the floor.

"Take the diaries," she commanded the men with her. "Search the study for anything else of his and take it all."

The god-headed men left her standing alone in the room with the mutilated corpse, looking down on her work. Youssef tried to breathe silently although he was sure she could hear his heart thudding in his chest. She turned her head and he pulled himself close to the wall, holding his breath but then he heard her step towards his hiding place and he panicked. Youssef ran down the long hallway away from the mummy room, fleeing the horrific scene as her laughter followed him like a curse.

DAY 1

CHAPTER 1

Oxford, England. 9.43am

"You're not well enough to leave," the nurse scowled, holding the discharge papers just out of reach. "You need to rest."

Dr Morgan Sierra smiled, attempting to move the conversation on as fast as possible.

"The doctor signed off on it, and I'm feeling much better. Really."

Morgan felt that the nurse could see right through her as she tried to veil the pain in her eyes, but she was determined to get out of the hospital today. ARKANE Director Marietti had secured her a fast release when they had received news of the events at the Museum in Cairo and she wanted to get started on the investigation. The nurse nodded.

"Then I'll put some extra dressings in your bag with the painkillers because you need to take care of that wound. You're not superhuman, you know."

Morgan felt the throbbing in the half-healed knife slash on her left side. She'd had worse injuries though and carried old scars from her life in the Israeli military. The memory of previous pain enabled her to endure what she was feeling now, and yet this throbbing went deeper. The man who had stabbed her had been transformed by a demonic curse and she still felt somehow tainted by his evil.

"Can I see Jake before I leave?" Morgan asked, hesitation in her voice.

The nurse smiled. "You can sneak in," she whispered conspiratorially. "He's still in an induced coma, but you can at least say goodbye."

"Thank you."

Morgan walked slowly down the corridor. She hated hospitals but this was a private wing and more like a hotel with attentive staff. The hushed white noise of machines and low hum of voices permeated the hallway and she wondered what news people were being told. How had their bodies betrayed them today? Her own was bruised and battered from the battle in the bone church of Sedlec, but she knew her limits. There was a margin of grace between physical collapse and a will driven by the need for revenge.

Her father had taught her that the warrior doesn't only fight when he feels like it, when the stars are aligned and when his belly is full. The warrior fights because belief and passion in his cause stir the body to action, for physicality is a mere shell around what the will can achieve. Morgan smiled. Her father had hated hospitals too. She reached Jake's room and paused, willing his eyes to be open when she entered. She turned the handle and walked in.

ARKANE agent Jake Timber was lying on his back with eyes closed, tubes twisting into his veins. His face was composed, the bruises there were only mustard shadows now, his cheekbones sharply defined by the liquid diet he was fed. Morgan knew that under the sheets his physical body was wracked by crushing injuries from the bone church. The coma gave him time to heal, but she could only see a shell of the vital man she knew. This body was not her partner, the man she had fought and killed with. Her Jake was in limbo, waiting for the eventual recombination of his mind and physical self.

Morgan sat down and put her hand next to Jake's on the bed. It seemed strange to touch him now, even though she wanted to, but they had maintained such a professional distance when working together.

Jake was responsible for bringing her into the Arcane Religious Knowledge And Numinous Experience Institute from the dry world of academia, where she had studied the intersection of psychology and religion. Now she was part of the living, breathing mania that accompanied these subjects in the real world. For ARKANE had given her a glimpse into a world beyond the headlines, where what she studied revealed a truth in humanity, an edge where spirit and science collided. ARKANE worked in the shadow space, dealing with mysteries arising from religion, psychology, the supernatural and unexplained. And despite how battered her body was, and how torn apart the knowledge she possessed made her feel, Morgan now lived to solve those mysteries.

"There's been an incident in Egypt," she said to Jake, hoping he could hear her. "It's Natasha El-Behery. She didn't disappear after Sedlec but retreated to Egypt and now she's committed a high profile murder at Cairo's Museum of Antiquities. Marietti's sending me because of our unfinished business with her." She paused. "And because of you," she whispered. Morgan took his hand and squeezed it, then laid it back on the bed and stood, walking towards the door. She glanced back. "I'll get her, Jake. Be well."

George Washington Masonic Memorial, Alexandria, Washington DC, USA. 5.47am

Maria Estes loved this time of day, when the streets were empty enough to walk freely, before tourists with clumsy maps thronged the city. As she walked, she gave thanks to God for her family and for America, for the new life she had here and for her job. She loved being part of the cleaning team for the Memorial. It made her feel connected to this land, where immigrants just like her had come to try and build something better for their lives. Although it wasn't one of the most high profile monuments in Washington, it was still visited by tourists every day and she loved to think of her efforts being part of their experience.

Those who traveled out to the suburb of Alexandria were certainly devoted to learning more about one of their Founding Fathers. Maria hadn't known much about the Masons before she had started this job but she had been slowly reading the information panels in the museum as she worked. She now understood that the Masons were a God-fearing, community-minded brotherhood who had acquired a bad reputation through scandalous rumor. For the great George Washington had been a lifelong Mason, as were many men of his time.

Maria had learned that at his inauguration, Washington took the oath of office on a Masonic Bible. He had sat for his official portrait in Masonic regalia and was eventually buried with full Masonic honors. And in 1793, as Acting Grand Master, he had even laid the cornerstone for the capital city of the United States, designed according to Masonic principles. Four US Presidents had since sworn their incoming oath on George Washington's Inaugural Bible, and Masons still held positions of power in the US government.

Glancing at her watch, Maria increased her pace, pushing herself up the undulating path that traversed the grassy terraces leading to the Memorial. It bordered a huge plaque with square and compasses and the letter G in the middle that she knew stood for Geometry, representing the Architect, the great Creator. She sent up a quick prayer as she scurried past. '*My work for you, Lord,*' she thought as she looked up at the Memorial.

Maria watched the sun touch the three storey tower, large bay windows reflecting its light. The classical facade was supported by six Doric pillars, fitting for the austere monument, the first of the three sections representing strength. Ionic columns in the middle section represented wisdom and the Corinthian columns near the top were for beauty. The cap of the tower was a pyramid with a flame inspired by the Egyptian Lighthouse at Pharos. It had guided ships through the Mediterranean into the port at Alexandria, for the Masonic Memorial was meant to light the way for the truth of the Masonic tenets.

Maria went in the back entrance, opening the heavy door with her key. She would be first here as usual but other cleaners and guards would arrive soon. She liked to get started early, preferring hard work to small talk, and she followed the same routine of cleaning every morning. Sometimes she found herself finished without even realizing the time had gone by, for the ritual had become automatic.

In the years she had worked at the Memorial, the place had become deeply wound into Maria's core. She knew intimately the temperature changes of the seasons, how the wooden artifacts needed extra care in the damp weather. She knew the characteristic smell of the halls and today she sensed something was wrong. She couldn't quite identify it but there was a hint of a dark atmosphere, resonant of fear and death. It hung in the air, a malevolent presence, and Maria shivered. Leaving her cleaning materials, she decided to walk around the memorial to see if she could find the source.

Maria checked the North Lodge and South Lodge rooms as well as the exhibit display areas, but they were empty and smelled fresh, as did the Replica Lodge where Washington's own Masonic apron and trowel were kept. She walked into the Memorial Hall itself, the polished floor squeaking under her shoes. Green granite columns supported the soaring ceiling and at the end of the hall, the huge bronze statue of Washington in Masonic regalia gazed down at her. There was nothing wrong there, so she mounted the stairs to the second floor. The smell was stronger here and seemed to be coming from the Royal Arch Chapter Room.

Maria loved to clean that area, for it contained a golden replica of the Ark of the Covenant and a gold menorah, as well as murals depicting the ruins of the Jerusalem Temple. It always seemed to her that God wanted her to clean it with a special reverence and she often saved it until last. But now she was afraid of what she might find.

Gathering her strength, Maria walked through the marble archway that led into the room, and froze in horror at what she saw, her body shaking with fear. The head of a young man had been wedged between the two golden cherubim on top of the Ark, their wings outstretched over the mercy seat of the Lord. His dark curls were matted to his head, his eyes bulging open in horror. Blood dripped down the gold chest onto the floor where his decapitated body lay spreadeagled in a pool of gore and feces.

The stench was overpowering and Maria reached out to clutch the nearest pillar. Her stomach heaved and she managed to turn away, puking up her breakfast onto the marble floor. Over the mural of the destroyed Jerusalem temple were words written in blood '*Shoah to the Arabs. Say no to peace.*' Down on her knees in the mess, Maria called out her prayers to God, asking for his strength to face this evil.

Oxford, England. 10.22am

Leaving the hospital, Morgan caught a taxi back to Jericho in the centre of Oxford, a combination of terraced houses on the edge of the canal squashed together against the stately homes of the old town. She passed the great gates of Oxford University Press, the entrance flanked with towering Corinthian columns, stone the color of liquid honey in the morning sun. It could have been one of the prestigious University colleges, the last bastion of old school publishing in the heart of the city.

The taxi pulled up in front of her little two-up-two-down house. The tiny garden out front was overrun and weeds were encroaching onto the short path up to the faded blue door. It wasn't much, but this was her home here in England, far away from the craziness of Israel and her past. Morgan unlocked the door, walked into the small entrance hall and shut the door behind her. For a moment, she just stood and breathed, enjoying the sensation of being home in her retreat, her refuge.

She walked into the living room and put her bag down. The corners were cluttered with old books, for one of her passions was to hunt through antique shops finding knowledge by long-dead authors who had attempted immortality through the written word. Her eyes fell on a photo on the mantelpiece. It had been taken one summer day on Brighton Beach and showed her twin sister Faye and little Gemma, her niece, building a sand castle. The sun gave their hair a shining nimbus, as if their energy lit up the sky itself. Faye's blue eyes sparkled, the violet slash in her left eye vivid in the image. Morgan had the same slash in her right, the only thing that really gave away the fact that they were twins. Faye and Gemma were her real family, but the people at ARKANE were beginning to feel like family too. Perhaps it had been the Israeli Defense Force that had done this to her. After so long, she hankered for somewhere to hang her loyalty.

A plaintive 'meow' broke the silence, as Morgan's some-time cat, Lakshmi, came in to greet her. Morgan picked her up and pressed her face into the soft fur.

"I missed you too. Was Mrs Dawes good to you?"

Shmi's rounded tummy was evidence that the kindly next door neighbor was doing more than was necessary. Shmi squirmed and meowed to be let down, for she would only allow a brief cuddle. Morgan knew that the pair of them were suited, each as prickly independent as the other. She looked at her watch. She had to be at the ARKANE office in the next hour which gave her just a little time to clean herself up.

Upstairs in her sparse, utilitarian bedroom, Morgan unbuttoned her shirt in front of the mirror. She gingerly pulled it away from the wound and examined herself in the reflection. The hospital diet and the craziness of the last few months had further streamlined her already slight figure. The lack of extra padding meant that the demon's knife had cut deep, narrowly missing her vital organs. The wound was an angry red around the stitches and bruising spread across her back and around to her flat stomach. Even on her mediterranean skin the darker browns and purple stood out.

She touched the stitches gently, feeling the edges where her body could sense something other than pain. It would take a while to heal completely but that was comforting in a way. Her suffering would last as long as Jake's, and when her body was healed, when Natasha had been stopped, then perhaps Jake would be ready to join her again.

Her phone buzzed with a text from Martin Klein at the ARKANE office. He was waiting for her at the Pitt Rivers Museum, so she had to hurry. Morgan looked back at herself in the mirror. Her dark curls were lank, her skin paler than usual and she needed a long bath and some recovery time. That wasn't going to happen anytime soon, so a quick shower would have to suffice, with plastic taped over the dressing. But first, there was something she needed to do.

Out on the landing, Morgan used a hooked stick to tug open a tiny loft trapdoor. She pulled down the ladder and climbed up awkwardly into the tight attic space. Putting on a head torch, she switched it on, then crawled along the main beam, wincing slightly from the pain in her side.

At the back of the attic space was a loose roll of old carpet. She reached inside the far end and pulled out the battered old suitcase hidden within. Kneeling before it, she opened it with care. For this was her external subconscious, containing memories she wanted to keep hidden but close, physical reminders of her life. Morgan touched the objects within, a sacred ritual she performed when she infrequently visited this confrontation with her past.

Her fingertips caressed two sets of dog-tags from the Israeli Defense Force, her own, removed after serving as a military psychologist on active duty, and Elian's, taken from her husband's bullet-ridden body. He had died embodying the leadership principle taught to the officers of the IDF, shouting, "Follow me" to his men as he had run headlong into a fatal ambush. Morgan touched the soft felt of her father's yamulke and a tiny shoe, belonging to her niece Gemma. The actions were her reverence, her devotion, her remembrance.

Morgan pulled a long sliver of bone from her pocket. It felt like the needle of a primitive race but it had been pulled from Jake's body after the events of Sedlec when he had been crushed beneath the body of the demon, Milan Noble. As the chandelier made of human bone had shattered on the ground, exploding shards had pierced his body. She had watched as Jake stood to confront evil, his face shining like an angel, but he had paid a great physical price for his courage. There had been another witness that night, Natasha El-Behery, murderer of innocents and still out there, causing destruction. As Morgan knelt there in the attic, she whispered a silent promise. This time, it would be an eye for an eye.

CHAPTER 2

Jerusalem, Israel. 2.34pm

IN THE PLUSH BOARDROOM in the opulent King David Hotel, Lior Avidan paced up and down. The terrorist bombing sixty years before had served to make this the most symbolic setting for peace summits and the signing of accords. It was the embodiment of 'we will not negotiate with terrorists.' It also had some of the world's most sophisticated security systems, funded by foreign investment cash and energized by the will of Mossad to protect the symbolism of triumph over terrorism.

Yet it was only six days until the President of the United States sat down at this table for the Peace Accords and Lior felt an unease that went beyond his usual concerns at such a historic event. His team had been through the security arrangements multiple times but the arrangements still didn't sit right with him. He needed to get to the sensation of separation he felt when he knew everything had been thought about, when everything had been planned for, when he had done his job correctly. Today didn't feel like that. Something was very wrong.

First, the phone call from Washington. A murder in the heart of the George Washington Masonic Memorial, the head of an Arab man on the replica Ark of the Covenant.

The death had been covered up and hidden from the media, for the Masons were lightning rods for conspiracy theorists and the press would have a field day with the Peace Accords so close. But it was the words painted on the mural that really stung him.

The Shoah was the term Jews used for the Holocaust, the genocide of six million in Nazi Germany. It was the reason they would defend Israel to the death, for they would not be annihilated in a homeland won by the blood and ashes of their ancestors. Sometimes Lior wasn't proud of the way his nation acted, but to use the word 'Shoah' against another race was to put themselves on the same level as Hitler. Could this atrocity really have been carried out by extremist Jews, he wondered.

Lior cursed and shook his head. Was it a warning or some kind of threat? Such a brutal murder was out of character for the usual anti-peace groups, represented by right-wing hawks on either side of the Green Line that separated Israelis and Palestinians. The murder alone would have been bad enough, but now a threat had come over the internet, gathering views with every minute that ticked by.

Lior sat down at the boardroom table and opened his laptop, flicking to the page that had been forwarded up the chain of command and examining the web page closely. It depicted an image of the Ark of the Covenant as it was marched around the walls of Jericho, hoisted high on golden poles perched on the shoulders of priests. The black and white drawing was so detailed, you could almost hear the blast of the shofar, the ram's horn. According to the book of Joshua, the walls came tumbling down by the power of Ark, so the image was Jewish, but a text in Arabic was inscribed underneath.

"A Sign of his authority is that there shall come to you the Ark of the Covenant … and the relics left by the family of Moses and the family of Aaron, carried by angels. In this is a symbol for you if ye indeed have faith."

It was a quote from the Koran, Surat al-Baqara 2: 248, not something that extremist Jews would usually be quoting. Then underneath in Hebrew were words from the book of 1 Samuel 4:5: "When the ark of the LORD's covenant came into the camp, all Israel raised such a great shout that the ground shook."

Beneath the words was a counter, the seconds ticking away as Lior watched. His team had checked it several times. It was counting down to the final day of the Peace Summit, to the exact time the President of the United States was due to sign the Accords between Israel and the Palestinians in six days time. Although the dates were widely known, the exact timetable for the signing was privileged information of which only a few were aware, so the leak was worrying and this strange threat a concern.

It seemed to Lior that the Ark was the one thing that would galvanize support in this city of contradictions for extremists on both sides. If the Ark were to fall into the hands of the Arabs, it would be a bargaining chip of astronomic proportions, or it would ignite a war in order to possess it. If right-wing Jews got hold of it, they would storm the Temple Mount and pull down the Muslim holy places to build the Temple again, uniting the Muslim nations against Israel and sparking a world war.

Whichever way he looked at it, the Ark could only bring violence. Of course, recovering the Ark was a crazy idea, belonging more to Hollywood than 21st century Jerusalem. But this was a land where ancient relics that could change religious history were still being recovered from archaeological digs, and Lior knew it would be best for everyone if the Ark remained a legend.

Lior had worked closely with the intelligence services, but no one had a good hold on who was behind this threat. There were plenty of far-right religious crazies who claimed to be ushering in the final days but these events had two unusual aspects, for no group had claimed ownership and even the best hackers couldn't trace the source of the site. The technical teams had been pinged around the world's servers through companies and government sites and private addresses but it was untraceable. Even Lior's best computer geeks couldn't take the page down for long, so clearly the group behind it was well funded and professional, determined to fuel speculation about the Ark and the Peace Accords.

The second problem was that it seemed to suggest both an extremist Jewish as well as an extremist Muslim agenda and on the eve of the Peace Summits, it was a recipe for sleepless nights. Ironically, Lior thought, the extremists of all religions were closer to one another in ideology than to the moderates of their own faith.

He sighed with exhaustion, running his hands through his thick black hair, for it had taken years to get back to this point. The last time they had been this close to peace was in 1993 when Yasser Arafat had shaken hands with Yitzhak Rabin on the White House lawn, and the two men had shared the Nobel Peace Prize. The world had expected that event to usher in a new era of peace and both sides of the struggle had finally breathed a sigh of relief.

But that was blown apart when Rabin was assassinated by an extremist Jew and Arafat later ended his days under siege in Ramallah. Even now, his body was being exhumed over fears of polonium poisoning, heightening tensions between the two sides. With the second Intifada bringing years of violence, it had taken twenty years to rebuild trust. Too many young people, his own children included, had grown up with conflict as their default position. Another upset at this stage would set the delicate process back another generation. Lior could not let that happen.

He pushed his chair back and rose to stare out of the bay

window towards the walls of the Old City. My heart is here, he thought, verses from the Talmud coming to his mind. *"God gave ten measures of beauty to the world: nine measures he gave to Jerusalem and one only for all the rest of creation."* As far clouds gathered for an oncoming storm, Lior shook his head, for it was also true that *"God also gave ten measures of suffering to the world and nine of them fall on Jerusalem."*

Sitting back down, Lior thumbed through a thick file in front of him, the material too sensitive to be kept digitally in a world of increasing cyber crime. There hadn't been any mention of the Ark of the Covenant from Arab groups before. It had always been American Christians insisting on finding the Ark here in Jerusalem. Like that crazy guy who had said it was under Golgotha where the blood of Christ had dripped down onto the Mercy Seat at the crucifixion. As long as they brought the right permits, they were no trouble, but this threat was new.

He scanned the data on right-wing Jewish groups determined to take back Temple Mount but the intelligence indicated that they focused more on protests and sudden violent outbursts, so this considered countdown wasn't their style. According to Scripture, the Messiah could not come until the Temple was rebuilt in Jerusalem, and the Temple would be unfinished without both the real Ark of the Covenant. With those prerequisites, they would be waiting a long time.

So why were the group responsible for this threat even announcing themselves, Lior wondered. They didn't seem to be demanding anything, just hinting that they had the Ark itself hidden away, waiting to be revealed. Lior frowned. This wasn't a police problem yet, as nothing had actually happened in his jurisdiction so he had no power to act. The website implied that an ancient artifact lost for thousands of years would suddenly appear in Jerusalem in six days. But the whereabouts of the Ark had been hidden for thousands of years, so how likely was it that this group could produce it in just a few days?

Yet Lior felt a deep unease, for the Ark was an ancient weapon as well as a symbol of triumph for the Jews. Could he risk ignoring such a threat? He had to do something but could not risk embroiling himself in dangerous rumor. ARKANE owed him a favor since he had helped clear up the mess at the Ezra Institute, so perhaps he would give them a chance to solve the mystery.

CHAPTER 3

Oxford, England. 11.13am

LIMPING SLIGHTLY AND FAVORING her uninjured side, Morgan walked through the muted light of the Oxford University Museum of Natural History. The neo-Gothic arched ceiling let in the sun through panes of glass, but even though it was summer, the light was dim. The skeletons of dinosaurs were thronged with children, their fingers caressing the bones of the long dead, chattering voices excited at their finds. The cathedral to science was ringed by statues carved from Normandy limestone, each supporting a pillar that stretched high into the vault. Here was Hippocrates, Galileo, Newton and Darwin, along with luminaries from down the centuries, fitting guardians of this cavernous hall of knowledge.

Morgan continued into the darkened atmosphere of the Pitt Rivers, a separate area of the museum. Torches were provided so patrons could see into dense cabinets, as the electric lights degraded the exhibits. The flickering beams of the occasional explorer could be seen between the high glass cases, giving the room a feeling of intimate secrecy. Here were treasures of evolutionary anthropology and archaeology, brought back from distant lands in the nineteenth century, when fewer questions were asked about provenance.

Morgan entered the maze of cases and although she wasn't here to look at the exhibits, they still drew her eyes. A squeal sounded behind her as a group of children discovered the shrunken heads. She smiled, grateful that a fascination with the macabre wasn't hers alone.

At the back of the museum, she pushed open a nondescript door which led into what looked to a casual observer like an unused store-cupboard. As soon as she was inside, lights flashed on, pulsed and began to move down her body in a full body scan. After a moment, the scanner bleeped and the false back of the room slid open.

Morgan stood at the top of a staircase looking down at the ARKANE base beneath the Pitt Rivers. From the central lightwell, five levels could be seen below, with glimpses of labs and investigative teams working on ancient and occult objects. ARKANE had taken the expansion of the nearby Bodleian Library as an opportunity and extended the subterranean tunnels up the road under the National History Museum for this hub base where they could take advantage of the vast knowledge and resources held by the University of Oxford. Morgan thought back to when she had seen this place for the first time, only a few months ago. Then, she had stood here with Jake, but now she was back on her own and everything had changed.

"Morgan, you're here. Come on down," a voice called up to her. She looked over the edge of the staircase to see Martin Klein waving up at her. He was ARKANE's designated librarian, a brilliant archivist, although what he truly did defied a job title. He took the secret knowledge of the world and mapped it into databases, then created algorithms to find patterns in the chaos and understanding in the void.

"I'll be right there, Martin," Morgan called as he ducked his head back into one of the labs and she limped down the stairs to meet him on the second floor down.

As she walked into the lab, Martin jostled over, enthusiasm bubbling, his blond hair spiked in a curious fashion where he'd been pulling at it. He pushed his wire-rim glasses up his nose as he beamed at her.

"You have to come and look at this," he said, beginning to walk away. "The amulet has a totally different inscription from what we normally see in the polytheism of ancient Egypt. Akhenaten is the key to this, I'm sure of it."

Morgan put her hands up in surrender. "Slow down Martin, I have some catching up to do. I'm fine, thank you, but Jake's still in Intensive Care."

"Of course, of course." Martin bobbed up and down on the balls of his feet, eyes focusing on the middle distance. Morgan knew that he wasn't so good at revealing his feelings, but she also knew that Martin cared deeply about her ARKANE partner. With Jake's absence, Martin was playing a more active role in the investigation, stepping outside his comfort zone of research, and Morgan knew his motives were similar to her own in trying to find Natasha.

She smiled. "OK, come on then. Show me the amulet."

Martin led her over to a lab bench where a turquoise scarab beetle the size of a man's palm lay on glass over a mirror so that the underside could be seen clearly. Its surface had been cleaned and there were hieroglyphics inscribed on the base.

"Obviously scarabs are quite common as they were used in funerary wrappings for mummies," Martin explained. "But this one is different. It's from the time of the Pharaoh Akhenaten, when he gave up the other gods and converted Egypt to monotheism for a period. He worshipped the Aten, portrayed as a great sun disc but it was a deeply unpopular change with the people. In fact, Pharaoh had to move his court to the city of Amarna, which is where this was from."

Morgan looked puzzled. "You're ahead of me Martin. How is this connected to the murder in the Museum?"

Martin picked up his pointer and stood at the wall screen,

his demeanor changing to that of a professor giving a lecture. Morgan felt the pain in her side throbbing, but she also felt the buzz of interest, her mind sharpening as she considered the problem. This was what she loved about working with ARKANE, the constant new challenges, secrets they could find that she could never have been able to discover on her own.

Martin clicked his remote mouse and the screen changed to show security footage of the Museum of Egyptian Antiquities as an agonized scream rang out. Martin flinched as black and white grainy film showed a man spread-eagled between two statues. Martin looked away as the man was tortured but Morgan forced herself to watch the violence unfold.

Martin's voice was matter of fact, trying hard to be removed from the sounds of the horror on screen. "You can see that the torturers wore head-dresses of ancient Egyptian gods. They are cult masks and from what I have been able to glean from the images, they are extremely well-made, indicating that they could be used for religious ritual and not just for this murder."

"Who is the victim?" Morgan asked, her voice sober in the face of his death.

"Dr Abasi Gamal. He is - was - the curator of the Amarna Period section of the Museum. He's written several books and a multitude of scholarly articles about the time and how monotheism spread in Egypt."

Morgan watched as the curator was tied to the sarcophagus and the knife plunged into the man's side. Even though she could only see the masks of the perpetrators, she knew that the falcon headed god Horus was Natasha El-Behery. She had seen the woman kill before and there was no hesitation, no flinching as she thrust in the knife. *I'm coming for you*, Morgan thought, studying the way the figure moved, etching it into her memory.

"Does this specific torture method mean anything?" she asked, trying to separate the gruesome images from understanding why the event had occurred.

"It's the start of the mummification ritual," Martin explained. "But of course, it was never meant to be done on a live human. The organs were extracted from within the body cavity and then replaced with linen and fragrant spices. The heart, liver, lungs and stomach were put into separate canopic jars, stoppered with the heads of the gods you see this group wearing as masks. The brain was extracted through the nose but as you can see, they didn't get that far."

Morgan watched, bile rising in her throat as the final chisel thrust burst out of the top of the man's head. The masks obstructed the face of the murderer but she knew Natasha's eyes would be hard, without a trace of empathy. Morgan watched the scene to its end, for she would not turn away from the murder, nor would she turn from the task ahead of her. Finally, it finished and the screen went black. There was silence for a moment.

"What have you found out about Natasha El-Behery?" Morgan finally asked.

Martin brought up the files and Natasha's striking face filled the wall screen. She had the looks of a supermodel, but her eyes were as dead as a mannequin in a shop window.

"Her family are Egyptian aristocracy," Martin said. "Her grandfather even provided men for digs alongside Howard Carter, the archaeologist of Tutankhamun's tomb. Unofficially, her grandfather lined his pockets with the sale of antiquities to the West, stripping the tombs for artifacts that he sold to collectors." Morgan raised an eyebrow. That was some heritage.

"Natasha's father later became a great benefactor," Martin continued, "restoring the ancient heritage of Egypt and piling money into attracting tourists even with the escalation in political difficulties. But we suspect the funding for his business came from shadier dealings, a global expansion in antiquity smuggling. There's evidence to suggest he was one of the consortium that broke up the assets of the Baghdad museum after the invasion and arranged theft for hire on specific antiquities. He died five years ago and after his death, Natasha moved to Europe, breaking all ties with her family. Eventually she emerged as a key part of Milan Noble's Thanatos movement and you know well how that ended."

The screen faded into a picture of Natasha with Milan Noble in resplendent black tie against a backdrop of the Vienna State Opera House. They made a gorgeous couple, but Morgan couldn't shake the image of the twisted demonic figure that Milan had become in the last hour of his cursed life.

"Now there's chatter that Natasha has become a gun-for-hire," Martin said, "a freelancer with ties into the underworld of terrorism and antiquities smuggling."

Morgan nodded. "With her background and contacts, she'd make an excellent choice." Her eyes narrowed in determination. "I want to bring her in, Martin. She's the last of the links to what happened to Jake, and I know what she's capable of doing. What did they take from the museum after the murder?"

Martin flicked the screen back to the photos from the murder. "They took everything from Gamal's study including the curator's notes and some of his books."

Morgan pointed to where the body was shown in graphic detail on the blood-stained floor.

"There are footprints and the chisel is coated with blood," she said. "They left a clear trail of evidence and there must be fingerprints, so who's officially investigating this?"

"The Egyptian police," Martin said. "But they have already blamed it on the fundamentalist unrest that is sweeping the country. The investigation won't get far in a climate of political upheaval because the police are struggling to keep control and don't much care about the murder of an obscure academic."

Morgan frowned, puzzling over how to proceed. "OK, so why did they want this information?"

"That's the intriguing thing," Martin said. "Dr Abasi Gamal has written books on Akhenaten and the origin of Moses and the Exodus of the Jews from Egypt." Martin tapped on his laptop again. "But the murder in Cairo is just one piece of the puzzle," he said, bringing up a montage of images: the severed head and the bloody words in Washington, then the website countdown and image of the Ark. "Your friend Lior forwarded these to us just an hour ago."

Morgan felt a brief pang of loss at Lior's name, for they had been good friends when Elian was alive. But after she had left her life in Israel behind, she had lost touch with many of her old friends. A brief meeting after the bombing in Jerusalem last month had rekindled their friendship, but she knew they had a long way to go to rebuild their trust. She leaned in to examine the images more closely.

"These have to be connected, but let me guess," Morgan said. "No one wants to admit they are concerned about something so inflammatory as the Ark of the Covenant during the week of the Peace Accords. On the one hand, the secular press will have a field day with the ancient myth, and on the other the religious right will be inflamed with fervor at the possibility."

Martin nodded. "Exactly, so we have to tread a fine line to make sure this stays well below the radar of any press in preparation for the Jerusalem summit, but also to track the potential location of the Ark so we can stay ahead of Natasha."

Morgan gazed thoughtfully at the image of the Ark as it was marched around Jericho, aware that when the walls fell before the power of the Ark, it sparked a massacre of the inhabitants. Every living thing inside was slaughtered in the name of God. Her mind was reeling, for this was no longer just a simple mission for her to avenge Jake's injury. Israel was her country, her blood was in the land and she knew she would do anything to protect it from this extremist madness.

"Jerusalem has always lived on the edge of violence," she said quietly. "It ripples with extremism and something like this, even a hoax, could easily spark an eruption. The Israeli Army have stopped fundamentalist Jews storming the Temple Mount before, knowing it would spark extreme violence. While the Arab nations fight amongst themselves, Israel is safe enough, but if they had a common goal, to defend or avenge the Temple Mount, I can see how this could end in war."

Martin nodded. "That's what Director Marietti thinks as well, which is why you're on a plane in two hours, heading for Egypt."

DAY 2

DAY 2

CHAPTER 4

Kiryat Malahi, Israel. 6.08am

THE EARLY MORNING SUN shone weakly down on the homes of the Falasha Jews in the settlement of Kiryat Malahi. The place would be described as a shanty town in any other part of the world, but people were shy of calling places in Israel by such third world names, even though the inhabitants were Africans airlifted out of Ethiopia in the 1990s. Avi Kabede sat in one of the basic rooms tapping on a slim laptop, his powerful smartphone a portable wifi hotspot, as he listened to the rhythmic swish of his mother's broom on the concrete floor.

She swept the meager property daily before preparing a simple meal for the men who had left before dawn to find work. Mostly they wouldn't have found anything, but they still tried for the rare laboring jobs, attempting to earn a few shekels for the family.

It was pathetic, Avi thought, but soon the Falasha would rise again and his brothers would have the prosperity they deserved. Once Ethiopia had been a rich country, a great and powerful nation, their kings descended from the union of the Queen of Sheba and King Solomon. Theirs was a noble nation brought low and Avi was determined to hasten the return of pride to his people, his methods based on stealth and terror.

This morning he was hacking into a news site, getting ready to leak the images of the Washington murder online. It had been easy enough to organize through contacts in the USA, but the resulting news story had been covered up. It was time to stoke the extremist flames.

Avi wore a traditional robe, his dark skin a contrast to the brilliant white his mother scrubbed so diligently of the ever-present dust. It was cool, but the garment was also a respectful way to honor his culture and the past. Avi had been just a young boy when the Ethiopian Jews had been airlifted out of their homeland for a new future in Israel, the promised land of milk and honey, a biblical paradise. After centuries of worshipping far from Jerusalem, they would be able to see the places written of in scripture.

Avi didn't remember life before Israel, but the twenty years since had seen the lot of Ethiopian Jews steadily worsen in their adopted country. They had never been able to claw their way into a society that saw them as so different. Ashkenazi Jews were recognizable for their white European heritage, Sephardi Jews for their Mediterranean looks, but the black skin of Ethiopia didn't fit. Avi had watched his community broken by murder suicides as hopeless men had taken their families with them to the next life, exhausted by the desperation in this one. Uprooted from the past, with no discernible future, some people just couldn't cope. It seemed that the racial nature of skin color would always separate the Ethiopian Jews from others. Equally, the tribal nature of religion would always separate the Falasha from the other African nations. So they had ended up here, but for what, Avi thought.

The revving of a vehicle from further down the road interrupted his thoughts. Avi stood to look out the window as it screeched to a halt at the boundary of the settlement, hip hop music blaring at full volume. A young man jumped out of the passenger side, running around to the trunk of the car. He popped it open and then hauled a body out, dumping it on the dusty ground. Avi reached for his smartphone, quickly activating the camera. He zoomed it at the car, clicking away as the young man jumped back in, barely closing the door before it sped off away from the settlement.

A scream went up from a nearby house as a Falasha woman ran to the body, her weeping echoing through the streets as people began to gather around. There had been other violent episodes like this recently, but the police largely ignored the poor black community. They were mostly out of work and subsisting on state benefits with no political power to change things. But not for much longer, Avi swore to himself.

He checked the images. The license plate was partially obscured but definitely traceable. He immediately began the protocols to route his back door access into the surveillance databases around the world, skills taught to him by clandestine hacker groups in China. Whoever those men were, they would be dead before the end of the day and the weeping of their own women would echo the cries he heard now. For the internet had become Avi's world, and online he could be whoever he wanted with power that most could only dream of.

As an Ethiopian, Avi could physically pass for one of the Sudanese Muslim extremists and this was the persona he adopted online and in his business meetings. In Israel, he used his Jewish identity and this was the origin of his codename, al-Hirbaa, the Chameleon. He was part of a network of extremists, men he had met in the terrorist camps of Sudan with links into the Al Qaeda network. But mostly each pursued their own agenda, for there was much money to be made in this new world of terrorism. The global financial crisis, the Arab Spring and increased political upheaval helped to camouflage what was going on behind the news, an on-going battle for the Middle East.

When he had presented a business case to his financial backers in Iran, they had laughed when he had talked about the Ark. *"How can it possibly be found in such a short time?"* they had asked, for it had been lost for millennia. But he had convinced them with new studies and fresh leads, and the need to take a risk. For if Jerusalem went crazy during the Summit, the collateral damage would be considerable. He would whip up such a storm that the extremist Jews of Jerusalem would storm the Temple Mount to replace the Ark on the site of the Temple. It would spark a riot from the Muslims protecting it and with the tinderbox of international politics, it would be the catalyst to the next world war.

The terrorist organization had discussed the usual possibility of nuclear attacks on Israel, but it would be far easier, and perhaps more satisfying, to implode the country from within. For if extremist Jews stormed the el-Aqsa compound with the Ark of the Covenant and the intention of building a Third Temple, the Arab world would finally unite against them.

Avi's phone rang. He rapidly activated the anti-tracking and voice alteration software before he clicked to answer. Natasha El-Behery's voice was calm and controlled.

"It seems we're missing some information."

Avi stayed silent. Seconds ticked by as he waited for more, a tactic he used to intimidate. Eventually it worked, as Natasha spoke again into the void.

"We can retrieve what we need," she said, "but it will mean another trip to the Museum. It will be risky, given that security will be improved after the last attack."

"Do it," Avi said in Egyptian Arabic. "You're already late and the schedule cannot be compromised. You accepted an accelerated timeline for the bonus payment so I expect fast results."

Avi ended the call as the brush of his mother's broom

returned once more to its rhythm. He had found the perfect freelancer in Natasha El-Behery, someone skilled and passionate but also crazy enough to try what others thought impossible. He had met her at an extremist camp in the desert of Nubia in northern Sudan. She was hard and fearless, definitely on the edge of sanity. He remembered how one evening at the camp a man had told Natasha that she had no right to be there. She was a woman, unclean and useless. Without a word, she had turned away and the man thought he had won, laughing and gloating at her, making obscene gestures towards his crotch.

But then she had turned back, grabbing a machete and with a swinging blow, cut off his gesticulating hand. He had howled with shock and pain as the blood spurted from his wrist and he fell to his knees clutching at his wound, but she didn't stop there. Shoving him backwards with her boot, she had impassively set to work with the machete, hacking his limbs from his body while he still lived. She didn't speak, she didn't flinch, as blood spattered her face and fatigues, turning her into a berserker of ancient times, a warrior consumed by blood lust. The sound of the man's moaning was soon lost in the dull hacking of the machete and her heavy breathing, but no one tried to stop her. There were no rules in the desert camp of extremist loners.

When there were only gory lumps of flesh left, she held up the man's head and spun around to the onlookers. One of the senior instructors started a slow clap and she had bowed slightly towards him. After that Natasha was respected and feared by the other men and Avi knew that this single act had established her reputation for ruthlessness. She had disappeared off the terrorist grid for a while, apparently caught up with some European project but now it seemed she was back in the Middle East.

So when his plans had been approved and funded, he had thought immediately of Natasha. Her father had been an archaeologist, her grandfather an antiquities dealer. She had the contacts but also the sufficient backbone to help him to achieve his goal, although he preferred to remain an unknown coordinator to her and keep her at arm's length.

Avi turned his attention back to the news site, for he needed to release the still images of the murdered Arab youth and the video of the beheading, which he knew would go viral on the extremist sites. It was time to start feeding a media storm and he would stir up the city like a hornet's nest. For in Jerusalem, there were always people on the edge of violence, those whose daily lives crushed them into mediocrity, but who, given a cause, would find the energy to rise up. Then the Falasha, his people, would go back to Ethiopia, triumphant, when Israel was dust.

CHAPTER 5

Cairo, Egypt. 5.16am

IT WAS SHORTLY AFTER dawn and Cairo was already gridlocked. Morgan felt disheveled from the flight but she wanted to view the scene before things changed too much, so the taxi inched her towards the Museum. She opened the window for some air, but the smog of exhaust fumes mingling with the smell of a polluted city gave her no relief. She shut it again rapidly. With over twenty million people crammed into high rise flats, slums and high density housing, Cairo was now the largest city in Africa. It was a diverse mix of people and culture, always on the edge of chaos, but also a city of dreams, where people fought for democracy against tyranny that had lasted for generations.

The motorway was packed, with donkey carts and motorbikes joining the throng of cars and trucks. In front of them, a cart piled high with cauliflowers teetered with every lurch forward to stay in the queue. It seemed incredible to Morgan that behind this mass of poverty was a city that had stood for over a thousand years. Cairo was called the City of Minarets for its Islamic architecture, but before that had stood the great metropolis of ancient Egypt, far removed from the modernity Morgan could see sprawled before her.

Finally the taxi pulled up in front of the Museum of

Egyptian Antiquities. Morgan paid the fare and turned to look at this famous landmark, a museum that had inspired many young archaeologists. She remembered how her father had talked of this place, where dreams of ancient civilizations touched the vaulted ceilings and the nightmares of dead gods lay in the shadows beneath. The building was the color of faded flamingoes, lit by the sun, a dull nicotine yellow, filtered through the smog of the city. Its funding had been stopped, as a new museum was being constructed near the pyramids, so this place was decaying even as a new one sprang to life. It was how Egypt had always been.

Morgan walked towards the imposing Neo-Classical entrance between the chipped sphinx statues, their mouths open to ask the traveler the ancient riddle of passage. Security guards sat drinking 'qahweh', the thick dark coffee that fueled Cairo. One raised a hand to greet her but they seemed uncaring of protocol or unconcerned about intruders, despite the murder in the museum and unrest in the city.

"Dr Sierra," a warm voice called from the museum porch.

Morgan looked up to see a slim man in a cream linen suit with a striped shirt coming down the steps. With his black skin and lively eyes, she knew this must be Julius Kagame. He reached out his hand and she offered hers in return. His handshake was firm, his eyes meeting hers and she could feel his wiry strength even though he was only slightly taller than her.

"Jake has told me all about you," he said with a grin.

"All bad, I hope," Morgan smiled back.

"Not at all, but I'm sorry to say that I may be a poor substitute as a partner. Jake has all the brawn, but perhaps I have the brains?"

"You're the local ARKANE liaison?" Morgan asked.

"Yes, I'm one of the agents here in Africa, although I'm usually based in the sub-Saharan countries. My rusty Arabic needed an airing and I wanted to be part of this for personal reasons." Julius looked grave. "Is Jake still in a coma?"

Morgan nodded. "But I'm determined that I'll be there to tell him we've got Natasha El-Behery when he wakes up."

Julius shook his head, sadness in his eyes. "Jake is like a brother to me and we have history from before ARKANE. I owe him my life, so I asked to be the one to help you on this project. Together we'll find this woman."

Julius's hands clenched, a nerve in his jaw twitching as he spoke, and Morgan could see that his passion for revenge matched her own.

"Is the murder scene still intact?" she asked, keen to get inside.

"This way," Julius said, leading her up the steps into the Museum. "They've taken the body away and cleaned up the blood but it's easy to see what happened, especially given the video footage. Come in, and I'll show you."

Given the spectacular objects inside the museum and the thousands of years of cultural history within, Morgan had been expecting a pristine environment. But this was Cairo, and the wealth of priceless ancient objects didn't translate into practical cash for such preservation. Instead, the museum was disorganized and cluttered, with millions of objects displayed in a seemingly haphazard manner. It smelt musty, as if the dust of years still lay upon them.

Julius led the way and their footsteps echoed through the empty building.

"It's still closed to the public," he whispered, the atmosphere sobering. "But there have been leaks of what happened and rumors of evil that has been stirred up, so no one wants to visit anyway."

"Why is it all so cluttered?" Morgan asked as she stopped

and gently wiped a layer of dust from the top of a display case. There were labels in spindly writing on some of the objects but others just lay there, as if discarded in an old drawer.

"There's so much here," Julius said, "They just don't know what to do with it all. But come, I'll show you the Akhenaten room where the murder was committed."

Passing through the great entrance hall, they entered a side room which Morgan recognized from the video footage. The smell of bleach hung in the air but it couldn't completely mask the coppery tang of blood and the stench of emptied bowels that caught the back of the throat. Lights had been set up around the sarcophagus in the middle of the room, which was still stained with blood and body fluids where the gore had only been superficially removed.

Julius pointed at the staining. "They can't just scrub it all off, because the sarcophagus is over 3000 years old."

Morgan shivered. How many more of the dead in the museum were victims of such brutality? Increasingly she was beginning to feel that violence was just a part of being human, that death was just a moment of pain in a life full of it. She turned to Julius.

"Natasha carved an ankh symbol into the victim's chest. Is that important?"

A new voice answered her from behind. "It's one of the most well known ancient Egyptian symbols." Morgan turned to see a figure in the doorway, silhouetted against the light of the morning sun.

"It represents eternal life," the man continued, "but also perhaps the shape of the river Nile with the delta in the north. It's still preserved in the form of the Egyptian Coptic cross."

He stepped fully into the room and Morgan saw him clearly for the first time. With a rash of dark stubble and wearing a creased jacket over a faded t-shirt, he was a modern incarnation of the Egyptian kings chiseled in marble close by. Julius walked forward to grasp the man's hand in greeting and introduced him to Morgan.

"This is Dr Khaled El-Souid. He worked closely with the late curator on the Akhenaten period. Khal, this is Dr Morgan Sierra, specialist in the psychology of religion and my partner from ARKANE on this case."

Khal stepped forward and extended his hand, which Morgan shook in greeting.

"I apologize for the interruption, Dr Sierra, but I heard your voices from my office and I want to help you find the murderer of my friend. Abasi was much more than a mentor to me."

He spoke confidently in English with the hint of an American accent.

"You were speaking about the ankh symbol?" Morgan reminded him, trying not to be distracted by his movie-star looks.

"Of course. Interestingly, it's also used today by the followers of the neo-paganist movement of Kemetism, who believe in reconstructing ancient Egyptian religion. You know, Egypt was a great empire once and we shall be again, or something along those lines."

Morgan raised an eyebrow. "The woman who murdered your friend, Natasha El-Behery, referred to the need for sacrifice. Could that be related somehow to these Kemetists?"

Khal shook his head. "I don't think so, as they are generally considered harmless. Although there are rumors of a more fundamentalist sect that still enact the rituals of the ancients."

Julius pulled out his smart phone.

"I'll get Martin looking into it immediately," he said. "Perhaps he can find a link between this group and Natasha El-Behery."

"It might explain the mode of the murder but not the

reason why. Can you tell me what Dr Gamal was working on specifically?" Morgan asked.

Khal walked slowly to the sarcophagus and put his hand on the bloodstains there, as if to honor the sacrifice of his friend. Morgan could see his grief and pain as well as his need for answers.

"We've been researching the Ark of the Covenant for the last few months, as a spin-off from our Akhenaten research. It was a direction that might have brought us more international funding. These new governments have yet to understand the power of Egypt's past in the tourism of the future so we need more investment to maintain and restore the artifacts that you see before you."

"I'm not entirely clear on the link between the Pharaoh Akhenaten and the Ark of the Covenant," Morgan said. "Could you explain?"

"Of course." Khal seemed grateful to find some distraction in historical fact rather than dwelling on present misfortune. He pointed at one of the giant busts, a pharaoh with aristocratic bearing and sharp, slanted jaw, soft full lips and a slim nose.

"That's Akhenaten, known as the heretic king because he tried to change Egypt to a monotheistic religion worshipping only the Aten, a manifestation of the sun god. He moved his capital to Amarna and took control from the high priests. The period he reigned over was also characterized by a different type of realistic architecture and sculpture, with more lifelike figures and more humanity."

Khal pointed at a section of a wall painting where figures of women played amongst bullrushes. "Akhenaten's worship of the Aten was more personalized than that of any Pharaoh before him. The Great Hymn to the Aten was found in the rock tombs of Amarna and speaks of the creator god in a similar way to the biblical scriptures. But what is more important to us is that when he died, Egypt returned to polytheism. His statues were defaced and his city left in ruins."

"So how does that relate to the Ark?" Morgan asked.

"We know that Moses was an Egyptian, but our research suggests that he was a priest in Amarna during Akhenaten's reign and there discovered his own unique faith. Once Egypt returned to monotheism, he found a group of people who would follow him, the oppressed slave caste of the Hebrews. He eventually led them out of Egypt into the Sinai in the biblical Exodus. So it was Akhenaten who started monotheism, but Moses who transformed that into the beginnings of the Judaism we know today."

Morgan nodded. "If we assume that Moses made the Ark in the desert after the Hebrews had left Egypt," she said, "why does returning here help us to find where it might be now?"

"I was helping Abasi with this research," Khal said, "and we have uncovered even more evidence that the Ark was of Egyptian origin. Come upstairs and I'll show you."

Khal led the way through the halls to the Tutankhamen Galleries with Julius and Morgan following. He stopped in front of the death mask of King Tutankhamen, the young face resplendent in shining gold, inlaid with precious stones and with kohl black obsidian eyes. The statue wore a blue and gold striped nemes head-dress with the cobra and vulture emerging from the forehead, a plaited ritual false beard lying on its chin.

"It's magnificent," Morgan said quietly.

"The mask originally covered the head of the mummy, which remained in the Valley of the Kings but two of the coffins are here, along with other treasures from the tomb." Khal pointed towards other cabinets which held objects that glinted and gleamed with golden light.

"Imagine what it must have been like to discover all this," Julius said, his fingers on the glass and Morgan could see a schoolboy's passion in his eyes.

Khal strode down the aisle, "But the discoverers paid the ultimate price, the so-called curse of the Pharaohs."

"Press over-reaction surely?" Morgan said. "Wasn't the cause of death an airborne contaminant they all breathed in when the tomb was opened?"

"That depends on your belief," Khal's eyes twinkled a little and Morgan was unsure what he really believed. "'*Death shall come on swift wings to him who disturbs the peace of the King.*' That's a curse found on some of the Old Kingdom tombs."

Khal stopped in front of a huge glass cabinet, containing golden objects for the Pharaoh in his afterlife and the canopic jars used to store the internal organs of the deceased. The canopic chest was made of a translucent, almost luminous calcite, ivory in color and delicately fashioned into the form of pharaohs' heads. Texts were picked out in contrasting blue pigment with labels to identify the liver, lungs, stomach and intestines. The King's chariot was ethereal, light and airy on gold wheels with thin spokes and rims, as if the god king weighed nothing at all. Gold leaf picked out the intricate decoration, as poles stretched forwards for the powerful horses that would never run in front of this chariot again.

"Howard Carter discovered Tutankhamun's tomb in 1922," Khal continued, "and it was the death of his team that made the curse a reality. The financial backer of the expedition, Lord Carnarvon, died of blood poisoning within weeks of the tomb being opened and several other members also died. Regardless, it was the greatest discovery in the Valley of the Kings because it hadn't been looted by thieves, and it remains the finest example of royal burial practices."

"So what's the relationship to the Ark?" asked Julius.

Khal turned and pointed to the display behind them. An engraved chest the size of a small altar sat on four carrying poles. Upon it sat the jackal figure of Anubis, his slanted black eyes looking towards the distant horizon. As Morgan gazed at the intricate carvings on the side of the chest, she spoke the words from the book of Exodus.

"Make a chest of acacia wood, overlay it with gold. Cast four rings for it and fasten them to the sides. Make poles of acacia wood, overlay them with gold and insert the poles into the rings to carry it." She turned to Khal. "It is similar to the Ark, but what about the cherubim? And Exodus speaks of the hammered gold on the lid of the chest."

In the brief moment before Khal could reply, Morgan heard running feet and a muffled shout. She shot a look at Julius. He would know the sounds of this place better than her and he was reaching for his weapon.

"Get down," she shouted as two men ran into the room and opened fire on Tutankhamun's treasure.

The huge case shattered and a hail of glass rained down as Morgan instinctively turned away, shielding her face with her arm as she pulled Khal down with her behind the marble of Tutankhamun's canopic chest. Julius ducked low and returned fire at the doorway, bending and sliding Morgan his spare gun with one arm as bullets sprayed the room.

Morgan snatched up the gun and fired towards the doorway, her heart thumping as she tried to assess the situation. Clearly they couldn't hold this group off for long, and she began looking around for a way out, cursing that they hadn't anticipated Natasha's return visit.

"The alarms will have gone off," Khal shouted to Morgan above the din. "The security team won't be far away because the museum has always expected a run on the treasure."

"I doubt they're here for King Tut," Morgan said, returning staccato fire.

The attack suddenly stopped and there was a brief silence, before a woman's harsh voice called out to them.

"I want the final notebook, Dr El-Souid. I know you're there and that you still have it. The late doctor's notes clearly specify that it contains the information I need. I will let you live if you hand it over quickly."

Morgan knew that the voice was Natasha's, although she was concealed by the entranceway and out of the range of fire. She turned to look at Khal. He shrugged, mouthing 'sorry' as he pulled a battered spiral-bound notebook from his jacket pocket. Julius looked furious and Morgan knew he would have put more protection in place if they had known there was another notebook.

"I'm counting to five and then my men will come in," Natasha said. "You have no chance against automatic weapons and you know it. I *will* find that notebook and you will suffer a worse fate than Dr Gamal if I have to speak to you on more intimate terms."

Morgan cursed to have her enemy so close with no way to get at her but she knew she had to stay out of sight. So far, Natasha wouldn't know of her involvement, and she wanted to keep it that way. She motioned to Julius that she wouldn't speak, that he should answer. He nodded but she could see he was favoring one side and as he turned Morgan could see the blood on his shoulder. He'd been hit.

"We're willing to negotiate," Julius called across the room.

"One," Natasha called.

Julius glanced over with concern and then looked at his watch. The response time of the local police and security services was known to be over ten minutes and the guards downstairs were presumably neutralized, so they couldn't win this.

"Two."

Morgan whispered to Khal. "Have you studied what's in here already? Can we give it to her without jeopardizing our mission?"

"There are two theories in the notebook, each taking a separate route for where the Ark could be hidden. The

African theory follows the Ark into Ethiopia and the Sinai route follows the Egyptians. There is strong evidence for both possibilities, but at the beginning Abasi is sure that the African route is the more likely. It's only in the last pages that he reveals a new clue about Sinai."

"Three. I'm getting impatient here," Natasha called.

Morgan grabbed the notebook from Khal and carefully ripped the last four pages from it, pulling the little pieces of torn paper carefully from between the rings that bound it to hide the deception. She folded them, handing them back to Khal, who put them inside his jacket pocket. The notebook looked as if it hadn't been touched.

"Good plan," Khal whispered. "This will give her both options, but the emphasis is on the African research. Abasi doesn't say exactly what he found in the Sinai desert, but I know where we need to get to and these last few pages give us some clues."

"Four."

Natasha's voice was cold and Julius was looking flustered. "Hurry up," he hissed. "We can't survive if they come for us."

Morgan could see that the pain and shock of his wounded shoulder was affecting him, and she missed Jake in that moment. Together they had been unbeatable but now she felt alone.

"Five."

Morgan put the notebook on the floor and slid it towards the door, careful not to show her face. It stopped a few feet away.

"That's it," Julius called. "That's the final notebook. Now leave us."

A burst of gunfire erupted, providing cover as a man slipped out and retrieved the notebook. Then silence. Natasha would be examining the notebook. Morgan knew there was a risk of the missing pages being noticed but as the seconds ticked on, it seemed that perhaps the ruse had worked. Then the sound of running boots echoed down the hall and the team were gone, along with the notebook.

Khal sat on the floor and leaned back against the shattered glass as Morgan rushed over to help Julius, who was slumped on the floor, holding his arm as blood oozed out from beneath his fingertips.

"You need to get going, Morgan," Julius said through clenched teeth. "You have to find the Ark before Natasha."

Morgan nodded, looking over at Khal, who had pulled out the notebook pages and was reading them intently.

"I'm going to need some help though. Dr El-Souid, how do you feel about a field trip?"

DAY 3

CHAPTER 6

Aksum, Ethiopia. 8.16AM

AS THE SMALL PLANE banked towards the town sitting at the base of the mountains, Natasha caught a glimpse of low-slung buildings, dusty grey-green against the landscape. A land of fable, she thought. Her father had told her stories of when Ethiopia had been a powerful civilization, although most had forgotten that now. He had taken antiquities from the area, with hardly any difficulty since it was a place forever underestimated and misunderstood by the West. Yet Ethiopia was most likely the cradle of civilization.

Here were found the fossilized remains of 'Lucy', the earliest upright walking hominid dated at over 3.5 million years old and the earliest known stone tools were also discovered in this area. The West only remembered the images of skeletal children broken by years of famine, but Ethiopia, once known as Abyssinia, had been a great kingdom. It had been a naval and trading power that ruled the region from 400 BC well into the tenth century, the most powerful state between the Eastern Roman Empire and Persia.

Aksum was a small city in the Tigray region situated in the north of Ethiopia, towards the border with Eritrea. It was the only place in the world where the Ark of the Covenant was openly claimed to be kept, and the curator's notes had pointed in this direction. Natasha looked down on the land, pitted and scarred like the hide of a dinosaur that had died fighting. The plane lurched suddenly and nausea swept over her. She grabbed the arms of the seat.

"Are you okay?" Isac asked.

Natasha nodded but in truth she was struggling, although she wasn't about to show it. Isac Abdel Rahim had grown up in her father's house, the son of his most trusted bodyguard, so it was almost inevitable that he would become her own protection as the years went by. As children, they had fought each other in the yard, under the stern direction of their fathers and each had deep scars inflicted by the other. Yet Isac was the only man she truly trusted, and he had proved his loyalty repeatedly. Perhaps they felt a kinship as brother and sister, even though theirs had only ever been a relationship of violence. But how long could she keep this knowledge from him? Pregnancy wasn't something you could hide for too long and he needed to know, so he could protect the baby as well as herself.

Natasha had found out for sure a week ago. She was only eight weeks pregnant, so it could still go wrong, but no one need know until she really started showing. Her breasts were larger but she was using that to her advantage, for it distracted the weak men around her. She had decided to finish this mission and then retreat with enough money to keep her for a long time. She would head to Asia, maybe Singapore, perhaps India. Countries with first-class hospitals where she would be hidden in the mass of people, the best treatment with no questions asked.

But did she even want to keep the baby? Natasha knew she was still struggling with that question. The father was Milan Noble, a Czech businessman, transformed into something hideous in the bone church of Kutna Hora, the curse of the Devil's Bible made flesh. But his genetic stock was aristocratic and he had been a perfect male specimen before speaking the unholy words.

She had gone to Europe to learn from Milan about the Western assumption of power. In the Middle East, it was easy to take power by oppression, through fear, but Milan had a way of drawing it to himself, an innate nobility that made people want to follow him, and that was something she wanted. She used fear easily, but didn't slip naturally into charismatic leadership. The baby would be the last piece she had of him. She shook her head at the glimmer of emotion. No, she would get rid of it as soon as this mission was finished, for it made her weak and she just couldn't tolerate that.

She thought of what her father would have done at the news. He would have cursed and beaten her for becoming pregnant by a westerner, a white man, not someone of royal Egyptian blood. He would have called her a whore and banished her until the child was born, for she would have become a liability, someone to protect, instead of an asset who could fight. Finding the Ark of the Covenant had been his quest, the one thing he hadn't achieved before his death, when the shades of the people he had killed had come for him in the night. Finding the Ark would be a kind of justice, a revenge for what he had turned her into, a way to show that she had surpassed him.

Natasha turned her attention back to the notebook they had taken from the Museum, flicking through the pages and examining the detailed research carried out by Dr Gamal. It seemed that the Ethiopians had been amongst the earliest converts to Christianity, and the Ethiopian Coptics still remained a separate church to the rest of the Christian Orthodox world. The Kingdom of Aksum even had its own language, Ge'ez, in which the sacred texts were written. But despite the claims of possessing the Ark and the rich cultural heritage of this land, the political troubles, poverty and violence meant that few Westerners came to investigate further.

The plane landed at Aksum Airport, bumping along a meager runway strip in the middle of a plain that stretched up towards the mountains beyond. A Range Rover sat on the tiny runway, waiting for them. Natasha pulled on her mirrored sunglasses and headed outside as Isac motioned two of their men to follow, for they only needed a small team for this initial incursion.

"Welcome to Aksum," the driver greeted them with a warm smile and open arms. Isac stepped forward and spoke to the man in a hushed tone, giving him a wad of American dollars. Natasha and the other men stood silent as the man's attitude changed and a glimmer of fear crept into his eyes. He took the roll of dollars, briefly thumbed through it and nodded.

"Of course, sir. I'll take you there now."

The tires of the old vehicle threw up a cloud of dust as they drove into Aksum, the eucalyptus trees lining the road providing scant shade from the Ethiopian sun. They passed a man in a white *gjellaba* leading a camel up the street, and a young girl in a mustard *shamas* herding three goats with a thin stick. Neither gave them a second glance, for this was a town on the edge of survival where eking out an existence took all the energy the residents had. Natasha couldn't see how the Ark could possibly be here, for how could it have come from the gold plated temple of Solomon to this humble, poverty-stricken place? But she had to be sure.

Glancing to her left, Natasha noted a strange field dotted with granite obelisks that stretched tall into the cornflower sky. The driver saw her look and risked speaking.

"There are many mysteries here in Aksum. This field of obelisks contains the tallest single pieces of stone quarried in the ancient world, eclipsing those in Egypt."

"What do they signify?" she asked.

"Perhaps they mark graves," the driver replied, "but nothing is known for sure about them. Few scholars come here now."

The Range Rover pulled up in front of the sanctuary of St Mary's Church, contained within a walled compound at the centre of the town.

"The church of Mary of Zion was built in the fourth century, the earliest Christian church in sub-Saharan Africa." The driver's tourist explanation tailed off as he realized that no one was listening. Natasha stepped out into the dust and motioned for the men to follow her. Steps led up to the church and the whole complex was surrounded by a stone wall. A turreted guardhouse sat at either side of the main approach, but the guards who were once stationed there were long gone.

Olive trees provided patches of shade in the courtyard at the side of the church and Natasha could see a few monks sitting there, robes blending into the shadows. They didn't rise to greet the visitors but watched their approach with faint interest. She decided to start gently and pulled a shawl over her head, an exhibition of modesty indicating respect for the religious tradition that ruled here. She could feel her gun in the small of her back and its presence soothed her, but sometimes getting what you wanted could be achieved without violence. After all, she didn't want an international incident that mentioned the Ark until they were ready.

She walked slowly over to the monks. They wore faded purple robes, the color of aubergines that had sat in the sun for too long, and all had long, grey beards on old wrinkled faces. With eyes demurely cast down, Natasha spoke to the senior man.

"Father, I have come a long way to learn about the Ark of Zion and to pay my respects to the church." She paused, then looked him in the eyes. "I have brought gifts for your community."

She waved and Isac brought over a thick envelope stuffed with one hundred dollar bills. The old monk looked at the envelope and around at his brothers. One of them gave an imperceptible nod. The man spoke in halting English.

"We are pleased to welcome you here, my child. We appreciate your generosity." He took the proffered envelope and slipped it into his robes. Natasha was faintly disappointed at how easily he had given in.

"What is it you would like to know?"

Natasha sat on a low wall, while Isac and the other two men stood further back.

"How did the Ark come to be here?" she asked.

The old monk took a deep breath. "The Ethiopian holy book, the Kebra Nagast, the Glory of Kings, states that when the Queen of Sheba went to Jerusalem to meet with King Solomon, she lay with him and became pregnant." Around him, the other monks nodded their assent to the tale.

"Many years later, her son Menelik returned to Jerusalem to meet with his father and claim his inheritance, but the meeting didn't go as planned. The son of the High Priest Azarius decided to steal the Ark and leave a replica in its place so he stole the Ark on the return to Ethiopia with Menelik. Because the Ark could strike down anyone whom it did not bless, it was decided that God willed the move. The Archangel Michael protected the Ark on the journey back and it has remained in Aksum ever since. The wings of the angels still rest upon its lid, for God is with us and has not deserted us."

"Even throughout the wars and famine," Natasha questioned, one eyebrow raised.

The monk nodded. "Even so."

"And where is the Ark now?"

He pointed to a separate building behind and to the side of the main church. "It is in the Treasury. The Ark of Zion is locked in its own chest and there has been a guard on it throughout the millennia it has lain here. The brother who takes on the sacred duty to guard the chest lives with it and must never leave until he dies."

Natasha looked at the Chapel of the Tablet, also known as the Treasury. It was square with ornate carved walls ringed by a rust-red metal fence taller than a man, keeping it separate within the sacred compound. Windows rimmed with turquoise dominated the square structure, while roundel decorations and carvings stood out in the walls, geometric shapes in the brick. On the roof, a small dome stood proud with an ornate cross reaching towards the sky, and a faded scarlet curtain hung over the entranceway to the shrine. It seemed a disappointing resting place for such a great relic.

Natasha had read in Gamal's notes that the Ethiopian Emperor Haile Selassie had had the Ark moved there into the Treasury so that it would be more secure. She also knew that, because of the military conflict with nearby Eritrea, no one but the High Priest of the Church could view the Ark anymore, not even the President of Ethiopia himself.

"I would like to pray before the Ark, Father," she said. Natasha knew that he understood what the money was for but he hesitated before speaking.

"Indeed, you can pray there," he said, "but you will not see the Ark. It is only brought forth twice a year, on Epiphany and the Feast of St Mary of Zion."

Natasha nodded. "Even so, I would like to pray before the shrine."

"Of course, my child."

He gestured to the youngest looking of the monks who got slowly to his feet. Natasha could see that these holy men would not be around for another generation, and whatever secrets they kept would die of old age. The man shuffled towards the Shrine and pulled a key from his belt. He unlocked the fence that walled off the Shrine and waved her inside, holding a hand up indicating that Isac and her men should stay outside.

Natasha stepped inside the gate, pushed through the velvet curtain and entered the shrine. Inside, it was stuffy and smelled of the man who had slept and eaten here for many years, overlaid with the heavy scent of incense. It was a cloying, sickly atmosphere with no sense of anything holy, not like the awe and wonder she felt when she encountered the ancient Egyptian temples. But she had to be sure of what the monks really kept in here, for Abasi Gamal had never been able to look inside the sanctuary of the shrine. He had never examined what they had and the questions in his notebooks remained unanswered.

"Tadiyass," a voice called the Amharic formal greeting quietly in the darkness. It was the Guardian of the Ark.

"Tadiyass," Natasha said in return, and as her eyes adjusted to the dim light she could see the outline of a man sitting on a chair at the back of the shrine. He guarded a doorway over which hung another curtain. In front of him was a thin railing and cushions for kneeling penitents. Natasha walked forward, affecting a modest pose as would become a woman in supplication to her God. She knelt before the altar and as she did so she pulled her knife from the ankle sheath and hid it behind the long folds of her shawl.

Natasha began to whisper a prayer under her breath, not to the Christian God but to her ancestors and the warrior gods of Egypt. The monk leaned forward as if trying to catch her words and she fleetingly wondered what it must be like shut in here for so long, with no hope of respite. Was it worth the reward in the afterlife?

She needed to get the man to come closer so she forced a cough, and then again, wheezing with the in-breath. The monk rose, perhaps to bring her water and she slumped onto the rail, feigning the need for his help. As soon as he was within reach she grabbed his hand, gripped a pressure point and twisted his arm, rising into the hold so that he couldn't escape. With the other hand, she pulled the knife and held it to his throat.

"Be silent," she whispered in his ear. "Show me the Ark. Now."

It didn't matter that he probably didn't understand her words for there was only one thing in here worth fighting for. She pushed the knife slightly into his neck, drawing a little blood that trickled down onto his robes and he said something in Amharic, gibbering in his attempts to pacify her. She held him tightly as she stepped over the railing and walked him slowly towards the inner shrine.

Suddenly he pushed against her, flinging his head back to try and catch her face with his heavy skull as he escaped from her hold. Natasha sensed his move, this idiot priest with no real fighting skills, and his attempt was all the excuse she needed. Blood lust rose within her, the overwhelming instinct to kill. As he turned, she bent her knees and used the weight of her body to drive the knife into his side. His heavy robes blocked the blow and he swung at her with his fists, shouting for help as he struggled. His cry sounded a warning over the quiet day. Dogs erupted into barking outside and she heard shouts, but she knew Isac would keep them at bay and she didn't even turn her head to the door.

The man came at her again and she waited until the last second, calculating her move. Then she slashed at the only part of his body that wasn't covered by his robes, his neck. The knife connected with flesh and he clutched at his throat, his cries cut off by the gurgling of blood from the gaping wound. He fell to his knees. Natasha stepped behind him and pulled his head back, then used the knife to slit the man's throat through the wound she had already opened, blood pumping out, darkening his faded robe to deep purple.

"To die protecting what you believe is the seat of God on earth is a great honor," she whispered as his eyes glazed over. He would be with his God soon. She was panting as she wiped her hands on the monk's robe. The exertion hadn't been great and yet she was finding it harder than usual because of the pregnancy. She was glad that Isac wasn't there to watch because he would know there was something up. El-Beherys didn't make mistakes, her father had always said, they only made choices. She wiped the knife on the monk's robes and slid it back into its sheath. Now for the holy of holies, the inner sanctuary.

Natasha walked to the back of the shrine and pushed aside the curtain that the monk had been guarding. Behind it was an altar upon which was a casket covered by embroidered cloth. In the dim light she could see images of people dancing in front of the Ark as angels swooped overhead praising God. There were also paintings on the walls, black men carrying the Ark from Jerusalem to Ethiopia as kings bowed down before it.

She pulled the cloth aside to reveal a dark wooden chest, simply made with no carvings or markings on it. There were metal rings for carrying poles, but they were the only thing she could see that linked this with the fabled Ark. Natasha drew her fingers along the top of the chest. It had been polished smooth, but there was no hint of anything supernatural, and she felt faintly disappointed. From the notebook she knew that this was known as the 'tabot', and there were all kinds of tabots throughout Ethiopia. They were all replicas of the box that supposedly held the tablets on which the Law was written, but she had expected this one to look different, if indeed it was the original tabot.

Natasha shook her head. Why had she believed it could be here? Some of the nonsense her father had read about must have rubbed off on her. In Gamal's notes, he had mentioned wanting to look inside the Ark in order to check for the sacred objects that were within it - the rod of Aaron, the pot of manna. The likelihood of these being here was slight but Natasha intended to look inside anyway.

She lifted the lid and it creaked slightly, clearly opened regularly as part of the rituals when the Ark was exhibited. Inside was a gold cloth wrapped into a bundle, covered with embroidered swirls and geometric shapes. Puzzled, Natasha reached in and picked it up. A jolt of energy ran through her, a noise like a rushing waterfall resounded in the room, and she felt a sense of vertigo. She gasped, dropped the bundle and the noise immediately stopped.

Shaking her head to clear it, she pulled her knife back out and used it to prise the folds of material away from what lay within. It was a shriveled piece of wood, as big as a man's hand, with a patterning of gold leaf speckled on its surface. Natasha was confused. Could this be a piece of the original Ark? What was the noise and the strange energy it released? This wasn't anything she had been led to expect from the notebooks or from her own study. Could the Ark really have been broken into pieces? This relic wasn't the symbol that would unite a nation, but if there was some latent power still remaining in the pieces, she needed to find the rest of them and get them to Jerusalem in time for the deadline.

She used the knife tip to push the cloth around the shrunken wood again and then pulled off the altar cloth to use as another barrier. She wound the material around the gold and lifted the package from the altar casket. Turning back into the shrine, she stepped over the body of the monk and left the Treasury.

A howl went up from the monks when they saw what she was carrying out of the Sanctuary. Isac and his men had their weapons trained on them but they still surged forward. The old man she had greeted earlier fell to his knees.

"God will strike you down for touching the holy relic," he shouted. "You cannot take it from this place for He has given it to us for safekeeping."

Natasha stalked over to him, all pretense of piety gone.

She shook the bundle in his face and spat her words at him.

"This is your precious Ark? This scrap of wood, this pathetic sliver of timber?"

He fell backwards as she stood over him. The other monks reached out to grab the bundle from her but were pushed back by Isac and his men as shots were fired into the air. Natasha bent close to the monk.

"Where's the rest of it? Tell me or I will burn this, right here in the courtyard and you won't see your sacred relic again." The monk's eyes were fixed on the bundle. He was shrinking away from Natasha's vehemence but she could see that he still wanted to take it from her. Keeping an eye on him, she half turned and called,

"Isac. Bring one of them." Isac grabbed a monk from the throng and pushed him down next to her. Natasha stood and pulled her gun. Holding it against the monk's temple, she asked again. "Where's the rest of the Ark?"

The monk at gunpoint began to pray, shaking his head at the man on the ground. Natasha pulled the trigger and the monk slumped to the ground, blood running from the wound in his head, soaking the earth of the sanctuary.

"You are from the Devil," the old monk whispered, shaking now. "God would not ask this of us."

Isac pushed another monk down next to him so that his body would fall onto the old man cowering on the floor.

"How many of your brothers will you give up for the sake of this fragment?" Natasha asked.

This man wasn't as strong as his friend. He begged the old monk to save him, to let him live.

"Too long." Natasha fired into the back of his head and his body slumped down over the old man. Blood and brains spattered his face and neck and he scrambled to wipe it off, gore staining his hands, but it was enough to tip him over the edge. He babbled words in Amharic, pointing south away from the sanctuary. As Isac reached for another monk to be sacrificed, he spoke clearly in English, raising his hands in surrender.

"No more. Please. You must go to the Lemba."

Natasha looked at Isac and raised an eyebrow. He nodded. They had been reading in Gamal's notebooks about the Lemba tribe of Zimbabwe, who also claimed an ancient link to the Jews and the Ark of the Covenant. It seemed that the curator's research had been heading in the right direction, although he hadn't foreseen the Ark being broken into pieces.

The sun was high now. If they hurried, they could make Zimbabwe by nightfall. Natasha stepped away from the old man and he was immediately surrounded by other monks, supporting him and dragging him out from under the bodies of the slaughtered men.

As Isac pulled his men back, they kept their weapons trained on the group, expecting a last minute resistance, but nothing came. Natasha set off across the enclosure, her steps sure and firm, flanked by the soldiers as they double timed it back to the waiting Range Rover. A great wail went up as Natasha stepped outside the boundary wall of Mary of Zion, as if their grief at losing the Ark could no longer be contained.

The driver was shaking as they got back in. He crossed himself and edged away from Natasha as she sat in the front next to him, blood still wet on her clothes. She leaned close to him.

"Drive," she whispered, her eyes meeting his, the threat apparent. Clouds of dust rose as they drove back towards the airport while Isac made the arrangements on his smartphone for them to head deeper into Africa.

Al Jazeera News Broadcast, 10.41am

Jerusalem's holiest site erupted into running battles today. Tensions have been escalating following the release of images showing an Arab man murdered on a replica Ark of the Covenant, inciting extremist rhetoric on all sides of the debate.

Fighting broke out as Palestinian worshippers exited the Al-Aqsa mosque after prayers, a place also sacred to Jews as the Temple Mount. The unrest was sparked by two Ultra Orthodox Jews who managed to bypass soldiers and run into the sanctuary to pray. Since late 2011, non-Muslims have been banned from ascending into the Sanctuary in order to prevent such conflict, and non-Muslim prayers are forbidden. Israeli police are permanently stationed at the Temple Mount, mainly to prevent Jews from accessing the sacred area which was left under Muslim control, despite the city being under Israeli occupation.

"It seems that freedom of religion in Israel is only for Muslims and not for Jews or Christians," Moshe Aridor, deputy speaker of the Knesset, told reporters. "We cannot even pray in freedom within our own city."

Israeli police tried to pull the Jewish protestors back in order to prevent them from being injured but they also had to fight Palestinians who threw stones at the group. Crowds on both sides were drawn to the scene and other splinter groups from the Jewish side tried to storm the mosque. Israeli military used stun grenades and tear gas canisters to dispel the crowds. Tensions have been running high recently since rumors surfaced about far-right Israeli activists planning to enter the shrine in a mass demonstration. Officials have called for calm.

Security has been tightened in advance of the latest Peace Summit, chaired by the US President, due to arrive in Tel

Aviv on Sunday. He released a statement today indicating that skirmishes and rumors would not stop him from pursuing this most important of objectives, a settlement between the Israelis and Palestinians.

CHAPTER 7

Serabit el Khadem, Sinai, Egypt. 3.48pm

MORGAN'S PHONE BUZZED. IT was a text message from ARKANE Director Marietti.

"Violence has already begun to escalate in Israel," she said to Khal as she scanned the news from Al-Jazeera. Her frown deepened as she realized the location of the clashes, the most symbolic site in the Holy City, and she could see just how close the city was to all-out conflict.

Despite the long drive from Cairo, Morgan was feeling alert as they drove further into the wilderness of the Sinai desert. After the shootout at the Museum, Julius had taken responsibility for sorting out the mess and encouraged Khal to join Morgan. They were now following the trail east into the Sinai, even as they knew Natasha would be heading south into Ethiopia. ARKANE couldn't bring in another agent in the short time frame and Khal accepted the risks of getting involved. Besides, the two of them could stay below the radar this way, pretending to be just another holiday couple on the Egyptian tourist route.

She glanced over at Khal. He was focused on the badly pitted road that stretched ahead of them but with his careful handling, the car zipped over the kilometers. He had gone home to collect a few things and she had grabbed a few hours sleep, but they had left Cairo at 4am, the quietest and coolest part of the day. It was a crazy city and Morgan was glad to escape it.

"Not long now," Khal said, a bump in the road causing him to swerve slightly. "I've only been to this place once before, a long time ago as part of my first degree. It's stunning."

"So, what's its significance?" Morgan asked.

"It was one of the locations of the extensive mining activities in the Sinai. The Pharaohs and ancient Egyptians used turquoise and copper for jewelry, and pigments for painting and decoration, so mining was important. There's a vast temple complex here that dates back to 2600BC, although the Brits stole everything valuable, as usual."

There was a smile in his voice but equally Morgan knew it was true. The early archaeologists had an attitude of removal, not plundering as such, but attempting to save relics from what they considered a threat to the artifacts. Nowadays, of course, things were different politically, but that didn't mean that anything would be returned. Khal continued.

"In 1904, the Petrie expedition, sponsored by the Egypt Exploration Fund, was sent to survey the region and they found this temple. Petrie postulated that this was the place where Moses received the Ten Commandments and built the Ark of the Covenant. But the official word was that the site was at St Catherine's Monastery and Jebel Musa to the east, even though it doesn't correspond with the Bible's geographical references. So the records of the expedition were suppressed and only a few copies remained extant."

Morgan could see Khal's excitement.

"So …" she prompted.

"So Abasi found a copy of the suppressed manuscript and that's what the last four pages of the notebook are about. If Moses was indeed an Egyptian priest escaping from those who would bring down the monotheism of Akhenaten's reign, then this would be the place he would have fled to. The biblical reference to the golden calf is considered a reference to the goddess Hathor, depicted with cow ears. The temple here is dedicated to her." He paused.

"But there's something else. There are indications that this was a site of ritual alchemy, where the Egyptians transformed gold into a miraculous powder. That's really why we're here, because it may explain some of the mysteries of the Ark, and because Abasi had some question marks in his journal about it."

Morgan leaned back as they drove the last few kilometers to the temple, wondering how strange this search could become. The Ark was surrounded by myth and legend, but there was a kernel of truth there somewhere. Certainly enough that it was worth pursuing the clues in the time that they had. She had sworn to Jake that she would bring Natasha down, and if she found the Ark first, Morgan would go to her. But if she and Khal found it, Natasha would come to them. Either way, there would be a reckoning, and within the next few days, because the Peace Summit wasn't far away.

Khal pulled into what could be called a car park, but was really just a wider area on the badly maintained road. A man in a dusty jacket and trainers over his traditional dress squatted by the side of the road, sipping from a glass bottle of Coke. Khal raised his hand in greeting and the man slowly stood, watching as they got out the car.

"Salaam alaikum," Khal said, in the traditional Arabic greeting.

"Alaikum as-salaam," the guide responded. He accepted the envelope of money that Khal held out, then nodded at Morgan and headed up towards the ridge and the temple grounds beyond.

"Friendly guy," Morgan said.

"The locals are charged with stopping looters but so few

people come here, their main job is just to take some money for the nearby villages. He'll hang back and we can explore on our own."

There were no paved roads up the mountain, so it was a vigorous walk to the top. The place was a ruin with little attention from the tourist trade and they picked their way through the rubble-strewn landscape towards the cave of Hathor. Ancient stele and obelisks poked up through the field of stones and Morgan stopped to trace the letters on one of them.

"It looks like some kind of hieratic script." She turned to Khal. "Do you know what it means?"

"There's still controversy, even after a hundred years after Petrie came here. The language is unknown and the hieroglyphs are not from any known dialect, so this place is quite the mystery. The deepest knowledge of the ancients is still hidden from view, protected from those who would cheapen it for a few dollars."

His voice was passionate and Morgan wondered what else this handsome academic was keeping to himself. They rounded a rocky corner and the full expanse of the temple came into view. Above ground, the temple was constructed from sandstone quarried from the mountain itself, blending into the landscape using natural rocky features as part of the building. A series of adjoining halls, shrines, courts and chambers were all set within the main enclosure.

"It's this way to the cave of Hathor," Khal pointed, "which is where Abasi's notebook says the alchemical symbols can be found."

They walked into the entrance and immediately the temperature cooled. Feeling the chill on her skin, Morgan breathed in the air and let her senses widen. If Khal was right, this was where the ancient Egyptians sacrificed to their gods and where Moses ran to after the expulsion from Egypt. It felt reminiscent of the great tombs of the Valley of the Kings, where the bodies of royalty lay with their battalions of slaves for the afterlife. There was a sense of belief embedded in the walls here, even though those who practiced the divine arts were now long gone. Khal moved further into the cave system and they passed an upright pillar, then a limestone stela of Pharaoh Rameses I.

"These were clearly too big to be removed by the Brits," Khal joked again, trying to lighten the atmosphere. "Abasi postulated that Flinders Petrie actually found the alchemical workshop of Akhenaten and the earlier Pharaohs. There were finds down here that were baffling to the discoverers, wands of an unidentified hard material, what seemed to be a metallurgist's crucible and a considerable amount of pure white powder concealed beneath carefully laid flagstones."

"What was the white powder?" Morgan asked. "Some kind of drug?"

"That's the big question. It was known to the Egyptians as *mufkuzt*. Abasi's notes link it to mono-atomic gold that was made here in a laboratory workshop under the guise of turquoise mining."

"What was so special about the powder?" Morgan asked.

"It was shown in tomb paintings as being presented to the Pharoahs as a white conical shape and is known in the ancient writings as 'white bread' or 'Bread of the Presence.'"

Morgan turned from the carvings she was studying. "Bread of the Presence? That's mentioned in Exodus along with the Ark, also known as shewbread. It's meant to be offered to God in the temple. That can't be a coincidence."

"Exactly," Khal said. "But there's more. Recent experiments with mono-atomic gold have shown that it has remarkable properties. When heated it weighs less than zero and the pan it sits in weighs less than it did at the start. So the weightlessness effect is transferred to the receptacle which is, in effect, levitating. It's also a superconductor and could pave the way to perpetual motion energy and environmentally friendly fuel cells. It seems there is a great deal more at stake than an ancient relic. This powder could even have been the alchemists' fabled Philosopher's Stone …"

"Whoa, hold on there." Morgan stopped Khal in midflow. "You're saying this material can levitate?"

"It can cause the material on which it rests to levitate. Remind you of anything?"

Morgan was amazed, her mind reeling with possibilities and questions.

"Scripture says that the Ark is said to have that power. But what about the rays of light that are supposed to radiate out from it?"

Khal traced a finger down a groove in the temple wall.

"There are carvings in the Egyptian tombs which link the mufkuzt with a device that causes a ray of light to shoot out of it, like a kind of primitive laser."

"But that technology is way too advanced for that time, surely?"

"Not necessarily. There are other examples of what we'd consider advanced technology. For example, the Iraq Museum contains the Baghdad Battery, dated at over 2000 years old, showing that the ancients had an understanding of electric cells and energy storage. Five such batteries were discovered and actually, the description of the Ark of the Covenant is similar to an electrical capacitor."

"What do you mean?" asked Morgan.

Khal crouched down, took out a pen and scratched in the dirt floor with the tip. He sketched a simple drawing of the Ark.

"The Ark of shittim wood was described as having gold within and gold without - essentially two plate layers of gold, a conductor, sandwiching a non-conductive insulator of acacia wood - here and here," he pointed to the edges of the Ark. "The two cherubim of gold on the top could have acted as outer electrodes. Even with low electrical potential, it would have become charged over time, and the discharge would arc from the cherubim with enough stored energy to kill. So perhaps the Ark was a weapon or a place to store this precious substance that physically changed the properties of the box in which it sat."

Morgan sat down on a rock, astonished by what he was saying. She felt the cool stone through her clothes and concentrated on that sensation for a moment. It was difficult to reconcile an ancient idea that was so fundamental to her father's faith with a scientific element that had only just been rediscovered. Khal paced backwards and forwards. Morgan could tell that he was still holding something back.

"Go on, tell me everything," she said. "I need to know what we're up against."

Khal looked at her. "I want you to know that Abasi was a rational man, that he was a man of science. He was my dear friend, but even I find it hard to understand the final words of the notebook."

"Seriously, I want to know."

Khal pulled out the folded pages of the notebook.

"I have to read it to you because it doesn't make much sense to me either. It's a quote from a professor of quantum physics. 'Mono-atomic gold, or the fabled mufkuzt, has a gravitational attraction of less than zero and because gravity determines space-time, the white powder is capable of bending space-time.'"

"Seriously?" Morgan said, incredulity clear on her face. "People believe that stuff?"

Khal nodded, a serious look on his face. "There's even one theory that the Ark still exists at Chartres Cathedral in France, but that it sits in a parallel dimension owing to the elements of monoatomic gold contained within it."

Morgan laughed, the sound echoing around the chamber.

"I'm pretty sure that an Ark in another space-time dimension doesn't pose much threat to the Jerusalem peace accords, so let's just focus on possibilities for the physical Ark, shall we?"

Khal looked relieved.

"I just wanted you to know everything about the research, but that side of things is getting a little extreme, even for me." He moved towards the back of the cave. "Anyway, this is what we came to see. The most important thing here is this carving, which ties this place to Akhenaten and the period of the Exodus. These pictures were suppressed along with Petrie's manuscript."

Morgan stood and went to look at the carving. It was a beautiful outline of a queen, a cartouche set in her crown.

"It's Akhenaten's mother, Queen Tiye," Khal explained. "It's similar in style to the Amarna period carvings. There's nothing like this at St Catherine's Monastery but even so, we have to go there next, because Abasi found something there that he didn't record in detail. We have to see it for ourselves."

They drove on, and as the sky darkened and night crept over the horizon, Morgan began to feel the magic of the landscape. The rugged mountains stretched as far as she could see, primordial granite ravaged by wind and rain, the exposed rocks open to sand blown from the deserts of Arabia. It was a place made for demons, for the spirits of a stark wilderness. This was a place to die of thirst and exposure as the sun beat down on your back and the scorpions crawled over your writhing body. How had the wandering Hebrews survived those years, Morgan wondered, as darkening clouds cast shadows on the jagged peaks that fell off into deep ravines. The angles of the rocks would make climbing them an impossibility and they could hide anything, perhaps even the Ark.

"Look," Khal said, pointing through the side window down over a ravine. "You can just see St Catherine's."

Morgan had read that the official name of the world's oldest working monastery was the Sacred and Imperial Monastery of the God Trodden Mount of Sinai. The Eastern Orthodox monastery was now a UNESCO World Heritage site and protected by the United Nations, but its beginnings were gruesome indeed. Catherine of Alexandria was a Christian martyr sentenced to death on the breaking wheel, crushed by bludgeoning blows while chained to a spoked wheel. When she didn't die from the torture, she was beheaded, and legend says that angels took her remains to Sinai where they were found in 800AD by monks.

Even from this distance, Morgan could see that the monastery was fortified, until recent times only accessible through a door high in the outer walls. It was integrated into the rock from which it was quarried, blending into the landscape, a stone fortress. Behind it, Jebel Musa, or the biblical Mount Horeb, rose majestically above the desert floor, the granite mountain where Moses received the Ten Commandments, one of the highest peaks in the region. Morgan felt a thrill of excitement as she gazed upon it, for these monks hid many secrets. Perhaps here they would find a clue to the Ark's whereabouts.

CHAPTER 8

Zimbabwe, 9.28pm

Natasha watched the last light of the day touch the hills and then fade behind them. The dusty road stretched across the savannah towards the mountains in the east, where green foothills could be seen, an oasis in the parched grey. The road twisted towards the outskirts of the Gonarezhou National Park, where a guide would meet them. They had been driving in silence for hours, an easy quiet made simple by the years that she had spent with Isac, but now she broke the silence.

"Tell me about this guide, Isac. I want to be sure we haven't missed anything. We don't have time to waste here and the clock in Jerusalem is ticking."

Isac's eyes remained on the road as he skillfully navigated the many potholes, years of driving in crazy conditions like these evident in his calm demeanor.

"Our guide was born Lemba, but his greed is stronger than his tribal links. It seems he wants to be part of the new Africa as a wealthy businessman and not as a tribal elder sitting in a hut away from it all. The money we're offering will enable him to start anew. In exchange, I trust that he will lead us to the holy cave where it is said the ngoma is kept."

Natasha nodded. The ngoma was the wooden drum used

to store the sacred objects of the Lemba. It was carried before the tribe in battle and legend told that it had guided them on the long trek through the continent to their current habitat. It was carried on two poles inserted into rings on the side of the drum and only the priests could touch it, while anyone else doing so would be struck down by fire. Natasha knew that it matched the description of the Ark, and they needed to find it tonight.

If Isac trusted this man, she had no doubts, but this incursion had to be done quietly and without bloodshed. Ethiopia had been a mistake. She had lost control and drawn unwanted attention to their quest, so this trip needed to proceed without incident. She pulled out Gamal's battered notebook and checked through his notes on the Lemba as the miles lengthened and the sun fell lower in the sky.

She read that the Lemba were an ethnic group found across Zimbabwe, South Africa, Mozambique and Malawi. They claimed to be a chosen people, direct descendants from the Jews and, more importantly, they also claimed to have the Ark of the Covenant. A British academic had spent time with them chasing the mysterious ngoma and concluded that the Ark was an ancient drum, now lying dusty and discarded in a museum. But Natasha wasn't convinced by his conclusions, especially as he was a Western academic, bringing his preconceptions to the investigation. People often forgot that the Egyptian Natasha was still African, and she knew that the rise of this continent was only just beginning. She was sure there was an Ark in these mountains: the question was whether it was the real Ark of the Covenant.

The Lemba were true Africans but genetic testing had revealed that more than half the male population tested had Semitic origins. The Lemba also had Jewish aspects to their culture, with a priestly clan emulating the Cohens of the Jews. They observed shabbat, a day of rest and they were circumcised. They refused to eat pigs, and ritually slaughtered animals. They didn't intermarry with other tribes, maintaining their separate status, and even their clan names were reminiscent of Arabic or Hebrew variants, setting them apart from other African languages. The conclusion in Abasi's journal was that the Lemba were related to a Jewish group who may have originally come across the narrow strait between Yemen and Djibouti/Eritrea into Africa.

Natasha gazed at the horizon and wondered at the longevity of the Ark myth. Part of her didn't believe that they would find the Ark on this quest, as it had been hidden for so long, or most likely destroyed. She could probably produce any old artifact and it would still ignite the tinderbox of Jerusalem, she thought, but her pride in her work made her want to achieve her goal. Professionalism made her want to collect the extremely worthwhile financial reward and deliver the authentic Ark to the mysterious al-Hirbaa. He remained in the shadows, but she felt through his communications how much he hated Israel. The country was an ouroboros, a snake that eats its own tail, a perpetual cycle of violence. Just like her own life, she thought.

Natasha sighed, for a moment wishing she could escape and restart as a different person with a new life somewhere else in the world. Somewhere safe where there was no hideous past, where history didn't bleed and where feuds didn't go back generations. Perhaps Australia. Natasha thought it must look like this country, with open space and areas to roam and disappear in. Her own country was steeped in the gore of millennia, bones broken by slave-driving pharaohs, women beaten and stoned, and great scholars hounded out by imbecile fundamentalists. Like Israel, there was no simplicity in being Egyptian, but did she really want a simple life? Could she bear to be someone who sat on a beach reading a book while out here was treasure to be found and adventures to be had? She rubbed her belly, then felt Isac's eyes on her.

"Something you need to tell me, sister?"

He never used the endearment in front of others, and Natasha knew that he would keep her secret, but now wasn't the time to tell him. She turned, her eyes flashing a warning that he understood meant he must be silent for now.

"Nothing, my brother. But put your foot down, we need to make that rendezvous in time, for we must make it to Dumghe, the holy mountain, tonight."

CHAPTER 9

Dumghe, Holy Mountain of the Lemba. Zimbabwe, 10.42pm

NIGHT FELL FAST IN Africa, and the shadows had darkened to pitch before Natasha and Isac reached the meeting point. They drove through one of the main entrances of the Gonarezhou National Park, paying off the guards so they wouldn't record their details.

Natasha breathed deeply. The scent of jacaranda hung on the air and the sounds of the night began to emerge, bullfrogs and cicadas, the bark of hyenas. Huge fruit bats flew overhead, their wings inky black against the sky. The park was named after the elephant's tusk and, indeed, the giant mammals still roamed the area. Natasha felt strangely at peace, for death was so close here. She could just wander into the bush and it would come upon her, in the guise of the lion or snake, or even in the buzz of the mosquito. There were so many ways to die.

She touched the scars on her arms beneath the long sleeves she always wore. Cutting herself had been a way to tame her fears of death, and now it seemed more like a friend. It beckoned her, whispering sweet things in her ear, offering its cold embrace. Sometimes it was hard to resist slipping into that sleep, but now she had more than one life to consider. But could she really bring life from a body that was both wounded and a weapon?

A light flashed ahead in the darkness. Isac slowed the car and they came to a stop beside another 4-wheel drive vehicle. As a young man peered in the window, Isac pulled out a red checkered handkerchief from his pocket and showed the man, who nodded in recognition.

"Glad to meet you. I am Matthew."

Isac gestured to the back. "Get in. The money's in the rucksack."

Matthew hopped in the back.

"We must hurry," he said. "The guards will be relaxed tonight as there is a celebration at the village, and we'll have time to slip past them. That British researcher brought us international attention a few years ago, but now the Ark hunters have stopped coming and there is little interest in the Lemba now."

Isac caught his eye in the mirror and spoke in a chilled tone.

"But you're taking us to the secret place that the researcher wasn't told about, right? I hope we haven't come on a useless mission."

Matthew nodded. "Of course, of course. You will see the ngoma, that is what you're paying for. And tonight I will leave this village, so of course I will take you to the place where it lies. It means nothing to me anymore, for I believe we must move on. No more tribal objects and sacred history, no more colonial attitudes and patronizing charity. I am part of the renaissance."

Natasha was mildly impressed with his passion. Here was the new Africa indeed, shaping the future instead of being fixated on the past. Maybe that's what she needed to do with her life, but Isac wasn't so impressed.

"You still have a way to go, my friend," he said. "This new Africa may find itself ruled by China at the rate you're accepting their money. An Eastern master could be just as bad as the whites."

Matthew shook his head.

"The Chinese don't patronize us like the colonials. They understand we are entrepreneurs, that we are mobile. Look at Angola. Right now, their economy is stronger than Portugal. The Portuguese, who once enslaved them, are now flocking to Luanda. Angolan companies are buying Portuguese companies and the money is starting to flow the other way."

"Enough politics," Natasha snapped. "Tell me about the ngoma and what else is in this cave system."

Matthew nodded as he stroked the backpack next to him. The fire in his eyes dimmed and he dipped back into the past.

"The old Lemba think that the ngoma contains the very voice of God, that his essence dwells there and that we carried it with us from the lost land of Senna. The ngoma must never touch the ground and those who are not priests cannot touch it. Death by fire and smoke will greet the impure who try to take it." He paused. "At least that's what they have always told us."

"Who are the priests?" Natasha asked.

"It is said that they are descended from a common ancestor who came out of Israel, and we have learned this much to be true from the genetic analysis that was done by the researcher. But the real ngoma was hidden when he came and he was put onto a false trail." Matthew pointed ahead. "Turn left down the track after the next baobab tree. It is rough, so expect some bumps."

They travelled in silence as the Jeep bounced over the rough ground. As the path began to wind into deeper bush and the track became narrower, Matthew asked,

"You have guns with you, right? This is elephant country and lions hunt here. It isn't safe to be out this deep at night, and I thought there would be more of you."

Natasha looked behind at him, her eyes piercing. "We

don't need any other people involved, and we're good for guns. How much further is it?"

"The bush is too dense to see the upper slopes but soon we are coming to the foot of the mountain. Maybe ten more minutes. Then we must climb."

As the Jeep bumped over the difficult terrain, Natasha stared out into the blackness, her mind wandering into the pathways of the past. Finally, Matthew called a halt and jumped out of the Jeep, Natasha following him with the backpacks. He beckoned Isac to drive into the deeper bush so the car was camouflaged in case the Lemba guards approached. Isac climbed over the seats and out of the car, then they pulled branches down and covered the vehicle as much as possible.

Tugging on their packs, they headed into the dense bush with Matthew leading. The sounds of the African night reverberated around them, the chirrup of cicadas masking their footfall. The call of a night bird sang out every few seconds, as if keeping time with the progress of the stars.

They pushed their way through the trees and under-growth which tugged and ripped at their legs. The track finally started to slope upwards and Natasha was glad of the pull in her calves. It was good to walk after being in the cramped car for hours on end and she loved feeling her body stretch. The sheer physicality of the world here thrilled her - the smell of the earth, the potential danger of preda-tors, the possibility of being discovered. Being on the edge was what she lived for, so how could she even consider what others would consider as a normal life? It just wasn't her. She needed to get rid of the baby because she wasn't cut out for the maternal life. She had brothers, they could continue the family name, and perhaps she would take one of her nieces to the terrorist training camps one day, to raise a new generation of assassins.

Matthew held up a hand suddenly and they stopped,

silent, barely breathing. Voices could be heard ahead. Two of them, joking and laughing. Matthew beckoned them on quietly and they stepped more carefully. They had agreed not to use force if they could avoid it, since they wanted this to be a silent incursion so that they could slip away without fuss. Isac swung his backpack off and withdrew a leather pouch. He pulled out two syringes of fast-acting sedative, handing one to Natasha.

They moved forward a few steps at a time until they crouched, peering through branches at a small clearing in front of a cave. Two men were seated by a campfire holding beer cans with two empties behind them. Relaxed, but still alert, Natasha thought. She indicated to Isac that she would take the one on the right, and they crept around the outside rim of the trees towards them. She and Isac had worked together so many times, they relaxed into a pattern of behavior where they almost knew each other's thoughts. Positioning herself diagonally behind one of the men, she visualized putting the syringe to his neck, pressing the plunger and catching his collapsing body. She knew Isac would do the same, for they had learned this together and they rarely failed.

A rustle came from the bushes in front of the men. They stood up immediately, hands on their weapons and looked towards the emerging figure. Matthew stepped out of the bushes. The guards relaxed.

"What are you doing here?" one asked the boy.

Natasha and Isac slid from the bushes and at the same moment, injected the men in the side of the neck. The men both looked at Matthew, stunned, and then dropped to the ground.

"Why did you show yourself?" Natasha snapped.

"I wanted them to remember I was here," he blushed. "It means I cannot return, and I want the break to be final."

Isac put his hand on Natasha's arm to restrain her anger

and nodded. "I understand, but we must hurry in case anyone else comes to check on them."

Natasha scrambled up the final slope, and before the others could catch her she stepped into the cave. It had a low ceiling and a cool atmosphere with a stillness she relished, and for a second, she savored it in darkness. She began to make out the shapes of rocks and images on the walls, shadows she couldn't quite recognize. Then torchlight pierced the darkness and the harsh light illuminated the walls. The ghosts of shapes coalesced into paintings and she bent closer to look.

"These people are carrying something like the Ark," Natasha said, examining a group of silhouettes carrying a box on long poles. In front of them danced more men and behind, women ululated to the sky. It reminded Natasha of the description in the book of Samuel where King David leaped and danced before the Ark of the Lord. The paintings were old, but the colors had been renewed many times, the reds made brighter by adding layers, but Natasha could see the faded edges and wondered how long they had been there. The Lemba had oral traditions and priestly DNA, so could they really have the Ark?

"Come." Matthew called them to the back of the cave. "This is the cave they showed that British researcher a few years ago."

Isac followed him, ducking under the low hanging rocks. Natasha briefly stood alone, her thoughts with the people in the painting, carrying what they believed was the very presence of God. Then she turned and followed.

The second cave was small and stuffy, far from the air flow of the entrance, and it smelt of blood overlaid with a sickly incense. What looked like a large wooden drum was mounted on a raised platform in the middle, and around it were packets of offerings wrapped in leaves. There were copper loops on the drum for the carrying poles, which were stacked carefully at the side of the room, but this was no Ark. Even if the word Ark could be used to describe it, Natasha could see it definitely wasn't thousands of years old.

"This is the ngoma, at least the one we use for most ritual," Matthew said.

Natasha spun around. "What do you mean? Is there another one?"

Matthew gave a cheeky grin. "That's why you're here, isn't it? I promised you the real ngoma, the real Ark of the Lemba."

Isac nodded. "We don't have much time, so show us quickly."

Matthew walked behind the ngoma to the rock wall, felt along it, and then slipped sideways into a space that was camouflaged by the contours and shadows. He disappeared, then popped his head back out.

"Come, follow then."

Natasha looked at Isac. She could see the excitement in his eyes at this surprise, not that he would ever speak in such an emotional way. Perhaps they would find the Ark today after all.

Natasha slipped between the rock faces into the roughly hewn passage, Isac following close behind. It was tight, and even though she could see Matthew's torchlight ahead, this was not a place to be trapped. Thinking about it triggered a moment of claustrophobia, a sense of the immense weight of rock above her. The musty air couldn't possibly have enough oxygen to support them all and her stomach flipped, a wave of nausea crashing over her. But Natasha knew fear and how to face it.

From a young age, she had been taught how it feels and how to continue despite it. She had been through ritual burial and rebirth, put underground in a tomb for 48 hours, breathing only through a tube to the surface. She had been acutely aware that the guard who watched over her grave could be overcome, that she could suffocate and die there. She had fought fear then and overcome it by the sheer strength of her will. Now she would do it again. Silently, she cursed the thing within her and again she swore to get rid of it, for this weakness did not become her.

"Are you well?" Isac's concerned voice whispered beside her ear, and Natasha realized she had been standing still, her breathing rapid and rasping in the cave. She took a deep breath to still her fast-beating heart.

"Of course," she snapped back, turning sideways in the corridor and shuffling after Matthew's torchlight.

He was waiting for them up ahead.

"This is where it gets difficult," he said. "You must stay close to me as there are tunnels, dead ends and fake entrances to confuse people who don't know the correct way."

"How do you even know this place?" Isac asked. "Are you of the priestly clan."

Matthew grinned, his teeth bright in the torchlight.

"It was a girl, the daughter of the High Priest. She showed me as a dare, for the younger generation have little respect for these sacred objects. Come, I will show you." Three tunnels forked away from where they stood, all sloping down in slightly different directions, none tall enough to stand in. "We have to crawl from here."

Natasha crawled after Matthew into the cave system, breathing deeply to dampen the tendrils of claustrophobia that still threatened. She heard Isac pause behind her, and a slight scratching noise but she focused on keeping her mind in check, for he could look after himself.

After crawling for a few minutes, they took another side tunnel, this one with four choices, then another fork took them further down into the mountain. Natasha wondered at the size of this underground maze and how the Lemba could have excavated it with primitive tools. It must have taken many years, perhaps the result of paranoia on their part that people would discover this ultimate treasure.

Her excitement grew at the thought of what they might find. A cave system like this would perfectly preserve ancient wood, as it was essentially climate controlled, the same temperature all year round. She thought of Tutankhamun's tomb, sealed in the fourteenth century BC and yet the treasures had been perfectly preserved in the dry environment for 3000 years until it had been opened again.

Matthew suddenly halted and called back between his legs, since he couldn't turn in the narrow tunnel.

"Be careful here as we have to cross some holes. They go down to open pits that are impossible to climb out of, so we must go down the right chute to the ngoma."

Natasha repeated the message back to Isac and they crawled on, soon reaching the holes he spoke of. She shone her head torch down into the depths of one of them but could see nothing in the black maws. They smelt of emptiness and for a moment, she felt a pull of attraction to the black depths, like the feeling of wanting to drive into on-coming headlights. She crawled carefully around the hole.

Finally, Matthew stopped and slid down into a hole that looked exactly like all the others. Natasha waited a few seconds and then slid in herself. It wasn't too steep, so she pushed herself forward and down. The ground was rough enough not to slide and would be easy enough to get out of again when they had to make the return journey. It now occurred to her that the Ark must be small indeed to make it this far down the narrow passageways. Was this trip all for nothing, or would they find a piece of the Ark here too?

She emerged at the bottom and dropped a meter or so into a circular space. There was a fresher smell, so there must be an airflow carved into the mountain. Matthew lit a camping lamp which cast a warm glow over the room as Isac dropped down behind them.

"This is the sanctuary." Matthew spoke with reverence,

despite his earlier bravado. "That is the real ngoma."

Natasha walked to the stone dais, where a truly ancient wooden artifact was displayed. It was a large drum, made of hard wood with leather stretched over the top, and clearly the modern ngoma was based on this design. She reached out her fingers, anticipating the rush she had felt in the sanctuary of Aksum.

"You cannot touch it," Matthew's voice was high-pitched with concern, as he grabbed her arm to pull her away from the ngoma.

Natasha laughed. "Suddenly so reverent. But I don't believe in your gods."

She roughly pushed him away and placed her hand on the ancient wood. Matthew sucked in a concerned breath, as if waiting for the expected thunderclap as she was struck down by the heavens. Natasha felt nothing except a sinking disappointment for the wasted journey.

"See, there is no power inherent in this object," Natasha spat her words. "You give it power through your worship but it is nothing more than a wooden drum." She turned to Isac. "What do you think? Can we take this back to Jerusalem as the Ark?"

Isac came forward and together they examined the ngoma.

"It's clearly ancient," he said, "and a hard wood that has been preserved by this environment, but it doesn't look like what you would expect."

"Bloody Indiana Jones," Natasha cursed. "Everyone wants the gold cherubim on top, even though biblical scholars theorize that the description is from Egyptian priestly objects. It's unlikely that cherubim would have even been on the Ark in which Moses carried the tablets of the Law."

Isac traced dark carvings on the surface of the drum. "I have read that the Ark may be the same as the biblical ephod, a word that was never really translated. But it perhaps refers to a drum, carried by the high priest using chains that would leave the hands free for playing."

Natasha nodded, quoting a biblical passage she had read in the notebooks, "And Miriam, the sister of Aaron, played a tambour, or type of drum, in celebration after Pharaoh's forces were drowned in the waters. Perhaps it could refer to this type of instrument?"

Isac shook his head. "But this is not an Ark that we can take to Jerusalem. That needs to be a figurehead object, one that people will follow into battle. This is just not inspiring enough."

Natasha sighed. "All this way for nothing. It looks like you can keep..." As she turned, she realized that Matthew had gone. "The little shit."

"Stay here." Isac pulled himself quickly up into the tiny passageway and Natasha heard him scrambling as he hurried after their guide. Then there was silence.

Natasha sat down in front of the ngoma and calmed her breath, concentrating on the whorls in the dark wood and the movement of air over the back of her throat. She could lower her heart rate incredibly fast with this method and sit still for hours. This discipline of her body was something she had mastered when young and still relied on when she felt out of control. Somehow it slowed time and gave her clarity in the maelstrom.

A thought came to her as she sat waiting. She needed Isac. He was her only true friend, but could even he get them out of the cave's labyrinth? If not, the guardians of the ngoma would find them and they would be subject to some kind of justice. They could buy the tribe off, so she had no fear they would die here, but the timing wasn't good. She would anger al-Hirbaa if she didn't make it to Jerusalem in time, and being hunted by extremists out for revenge was not something she wanted. They needed to get out of here fast.

She heard a scrabbling behind her and Isac dropped into the cave.

"I followed a few tunnels back but he's gone. I'm sure he'll just take the money and run. Sensible kid."

Natasha stood, stretching her limbs from the floor. "We must be getting old, my brother, to let such a boy escape."

Isac shrugged. "No matter. He deserves the money for tricking us."

"But now we're stuck here and we have a tight deadline to meet. I don't want to hang about waiting for the Lemba priests to find us."

"Have I ever let you down?"

Natasha paused, thinking. "Never," she said.

Isac gave a little bow, as a servant to his mistress. "Then step this way because I marked the tunnels so we could find the way out. You taught me never to trust anyone ... but you have been a little distracted of late."

Natasha was overwhelmed with gratitude for his forward thinking and his dedication to her. She even felt a prick of tears behind her eyes, which startled her. These emotions weren't something she usually experienced so she shut them down, quickly regaining control.

"You're worth every penny I pay you, Isac. Lead on."

At her harsh words, she saw the light die a little in his eyes but Natasha pushed her own feelings aside. He was her protection, nothing more. Isac turned and climbed back into the tunnel, helping her up after him. Using his marks, they navigated their way back through the tunnels.

Eventually they made it back to the Jeep, where the back-seat lay empty of the money, as expected.

The moon was still high as they drove north towards Nairobi airport, and Natasha willed herself quickly to Egypt. There she would sacrifice and ask the gods for help in their quest.

DAY 4

CHAPTER 10

St Catherine's Monastery, Egypt, 4.07am

A RUSTLE IN THE cool darkness woke Morgan with a start. It came again and she realized it was long habits sweeping the floor as the monks walked to early prayers. She lay in the narrow bed and listened to the quiet footsteps, a scene repeated daily for hundreds of years as the faithful men called out to their silent god. Strange that it should be Christians who have a foothold here, she thought. After all, it was holy because of the Jews, because of their trek across this desert to the Promised Land.

She and Khal had arrived at St Catherine's late the previous night, and had been shown straight to their basic rooms, but now she was keen to look around. Morgan got up and dressed quickly, lightweight walking trousers, t-shirt and fleece jacket to guard against the chill of the desert morning. She pulled on her sturdy walking boots and then opened the door slightly, watching the last of the monks filing into the church to begin their prayers.

She slipped out of the door, walking across the flagstones with a light step, her breath frosty in the air. She loved the dichotomy of the desert. It could kill you with heat by day, and by night, with cold. Humanity had this hubris about physical survival she thought, but we are really just on the edge of dying every day.

As Morgan crossed the silent compound, she saw a tiny light shining from the Chapel of the Burning Bush. It surrounded what was believed to be the original bush, still sprouting, where Moses heard the voice of God telling him to go to Egypt and lead the Israelites out. Legend told that it was here that God told Moses "I am who I am". Morgan thought on this for a minute. There was no defining her God, but she felt him here in the desert more than she did in the city. Perhaps this was why people retreated to places like this. With no distractions, no cornered world to prevent contemplation, you could meet with God high on the mountain.

She headed back out into the cool morning, pausing at the gate of the monastery, the threshold to the wild. Outside was a hostile place, but one where you could perhaps get closer to the Divine, and that was always better done alone. She swung open the low door and ducked outside, pulling it closed behind her.

Morgan walked steadily up the steep slope of Mount Sinai, heading for the place where legend said that Moses received the Ten Commandments. This proximity to ancient places made her think of her own past, for she had a complicated relationship with Judaism, and being out here brought those memories and insecurities to the fore. As she stretched her legs she thought of her father. She hadn't been born Jewish, as her mother had been a Welsh Christian, her father originally a secular Jew. When her parents divorced, Morgan was taken to live with her father in Israel, while her twin sister Faye remained in England with their mother.

So Morgan was brought up in a country of Jews but the word had so many meanings. Some were secular, the bronzed Israelis of Tel Aviv beach, playing volleyball in the sun, muscles oiled and tanned, the type she was definitely interested in as a teenager. But she also met other Jews when accompanying her father on archaeological digs every holiday when he was a Professor at Hebrew University. At those gatherings, conservative and reform Jews mingled with the secular. The food was Kosher and they sang songs at night, ancient melodies of this very desert and the faithfulness of God who brought them out of Egypt. Then there were the Ultra Orthodox, the Haredim, whose area of Jerusalem her father had warned her to avoid. The men would stone her for her immodest dress, he said, raising an eyebrow at her tiny shorts and long, lean brown legs.

Morgan had entered the Israeli Defense Force for her National Service, and around that time her father had begun to observe the faith which he had put aside as a younger man. After a particular dig in Safed, he had began to research the mysticism of Kabbalah and, over the years, as she studied as a psychologist, he became a devotee. His little flat in Jerusalem became piled high with sacred texts and writings of the Kabbalists and like them, he sought the truth behind the words of the Torah.

Morgan had never joined him in the faith he embraced and so never officially converted. She could have made that decision at any point, but part of her was tied to a mother and twin sister in England, and she wanted to stay an outsider so she would never forget them. She thought of her sister Faye and her niece, Gemma, who would be sleeping in their beds right now in a little village outside Oxford. Her attachment to them had endangered their lives in the past and that gave her pause, but she wouldn't let that happen again.

Dawn rose in shades of peony pink above the rocks of Sinai, a cathedral of twisted and windswept stone. Morgan had started walking in the darkness, hiking up towards the peak to greet the sunrise and look down on the monastery. Now she climbed the Steps of Repentance towards the summit of Jebel Musa, Mount Sinai. She wheezed a little and slowed her pace, thrilling at the exercise but also feeling the strain as her injuries were still healing. She forced her legs onwards, overcoming the need to stop with sheer will.

The light was stronger now and Morgan could see the scrub of the mountain more clearly. Close-growing bushes and angular rocks projected from the dust like ancient monuments, half buried in the ochre earth. The occasional skitter of lizards was the only sound other than her footsteps and labored breathing as she pushed herself faster up the mountain. Perhaps her ancient ancestors had seen sunrises here as they spent forty years wandering this desert, a pillar of fire lighting their way by night and a pillar of dust by day. The old stories were resonant with hidden truth, rooted in the physicality that this desert held even now. Morgan felt the power of the earth beneath her and a desert sky that had enthralled generations, stars that had inspired the prophets and a land where a Chosen People had met their God.

A piercing cry sounded from above. Morgan looked up to see a golden eagle with a wingspan of over six feet, hunting for rock hyrax, soaring in the mountain air, majestic and timeless. Birds like these would have seen the march of the Israelites across the desert, she thought. Morgan felt myths rise and swirl about her, for it was a place of magic where perhaps the supernatural could manifest. The eagle swooped low and hit, then soared again, carrying its struggling prey to hungry chicks which would tear it to pieces while it still breathed. Nature is not kind, Morgan thought, as she reflectively stroked the scars from her own battles. As Tennyson said, it is indeed red in tooth and claw, for we are violence incarnate and human decency is only a facade to hide our true selves.

Finally Morgan walked out from behind a large rock and emerged onto a platform, chiseled onto the mountain top for people to sit and contemplate the heavens and the earth that lay before them. The desert stretched to the horizon, a rock-sculpted landscape of incised valleys and rolling hills, empty of human habitation, except for the monastery which lay tiny below her.

Morgan breathed in the cool air as her heart rate returned to normal after the climb. The warmth in her muscles began to chill as she stood unmoving, looking into the sunrise. Orange and pink streaks pierced the clouds and a ray of sunlight touched the desert hills in front of her. Morgan smiled as she remembered her father saying that angels travelled on these rays: perhaps one was riding to earth at that moment.

She recalled the words of Exodus, when God summoned Moses to the top of this mountain. Morgan loved storms, and her father would tell her this story when thunder rolled over Jerusalem and rain hammered down on their roof. As lightning forked, splitting the sky, he had told her how God came to Moses. Mount Sinai had been covered in smoke and the Lord descended on it in fire. The whole mountain had trembled with its violence but Moses had gone up into the thick darkness and met with God. Here he had received the tablets of Testimony, stone inscribed by the very finger of God.

Morgan shivered, whether from the chill air or the feeling that this place was indeed holy. For there were places in the world where the physical stretched thin, when the spiritual bubbled up and made its presence known. For her, Sinai was heavy with symbolism, impregnated by faith. She watched as the sun rose higher, pink and orange fading to a yellow that darkened and was absorbed into the slate-grey rocks. The landscape seemed to devour light, as if the demons of the desert pushed back against the sun, protecting their hiding places with dank shadow. Looking into the rocky hills was like watching shape-shifting clouds. It seemed there were figures hiding, abandoned cities, animals that crouched and leapt, slithered and flew in the shade of the cliffs. She blinked and it became an empty place again, where anything living was finding shelter before the sun blistered the land for another day.

Morgan turned and looked towards the final summit. The platform where she was standing was clearly made safe for tourists but there was a further climb with prohibiting signs that blocked the way. Faint markings showed where a rough path had been made, perhaps by people determined to find a more private spot to commune with God. She climbed over the barrier and scrambled up the rocky face, heading for a cleft in the rocks above.

Her father had read to her of how Moses had asked to see the glory of the Lord, daring to request a physical sign. So God had revealed himself, but as He passed, He had hidden Moses in a cleft in the rock because no one could look on His face and live. Morgan had always been fascinated by that story. How had Moses dared to ask such a thing of God? And what did His Glory look like?

She reached the cleft and slipped inside. It was wide enough to hide in but the entrance could easily be covered. Morgan smiled. If Jake could see her now, he would laugh at her acting out this myth. They both knew that there were things that couldn't be explained, and both had a kind of faith that didn't fit into any religious box, but both of them also had a healthy cynicism. She thought of Jake back in the hospital, the machines beeping around him, keeping him alive, and she clenched her fists. She needed to focus on finding the Ark and Natasha.

CHAPTER 11

St Catherine's Library. Sinai, Egypt. 1.33pm

THE DOUR-FACED ABBOT unlocked the door to the library with a heavy, old-fashioned key tied to a rope belt around his waist.

"Epharisto," Khal said in Greek, bowing slightly to the older man, who responded with a nod before leaving them to enter alone.

Morgan walked into the library, spinning slowly around to take in the scene that confronted her. Shelves of dark wood stretched away from them making corridors of books, whilst above them towered more volumes on balconies supported by thick pillars. The vaulted ceilings and supporting columns were a dull cream color, a backdrop to the dramatic expanse of knowledge displayed before them. A few monks were sitting at desks, large tomes open in front of them.

"Magnificent, isn't it?" Khal whispered. "I came here several times with Abasi, although not the last time." Morgan heard the regret in his voice as he paused, then continued. "It has the second largest collection of early codices and manuscripts in the world, exceeded only by the Vatican. There are over 3500 volumes here, in Greek, Coptic, Arabic, Armenian, Hebrew, Syriac and other languages."

Morgan walked to the closest rack of shelves.

"Is there some kind of index?" she asked. "We don't have enough time for a random search, much as I'd love to stay here and immerse myself in these glorious books." She ran her fingers along the spines, feeling the rub of their pages, letting the ancient dust coat her fingertips.

Khal walked around behind a bookcase.

"There's a computer here with a searchable index of the material," he said. "No internet access of course, but at least it's something to help us narrow the search."

Morgan started to walk towards him and then noticed an alcove with a glass cabinet.

"What's that?" she asked. Khal looked around and joined her in front of the case.

"That's the Achtiname in which Mohammed bestowed his protection on the monastery. Written in 623, it exempts the monastery from taxes and military service and commands Muslims to help the monks."

"Wow," Morgan said, peering into the cabinet. "That's pretty impressive."

Khal nodded. "It's also the reason why the monastery has remained independent for 17 centuries. It has never been attacked and the dry atmosphere has been an almost perfect environment for preserving these treasures. Muslims destroyed so much of the Christian heritage in the Middle East, but this place was spared by Mohammed himself."

Next to the cabinet was an alcove with a twelfth century icon of the Ladder of Divine Ascent. On a gold background, it showed a ladder pointing towards heaven with monks perching precariously on the rungs, walking the thirty steps of the monastic life towards heaven. Angels watched them from afar, but around them buzzed black demons with arrows and sharp wings, lassoing the faithful and pulling them off towards Hell beneath. Morgan felt a flash of pity for the fallen, for she knew this path of struggle, attempting to fly but being pulled relentlessly down.

Shaking her head, she walked to the computer desk, as Khal checked the notebook pages again. He tapped on the keyboard, began a search, then clicked the Print button. The dot matrix printer cranked into life and scrolled slowly, creaking as it tapped out the locations of books in the vast library.

Morgan raised an eyebrow at the ancient device. "I know they think tradition is important, but seriously?"

"There should really be an app for it, right?" Khal said, ripping the paper from the printer. Twenty-four items on the list were marked with the key of Exodus. There were versions of the original text and commentaries on the book, some Jewish, others Christian, with two by Koranic scholars.

"So where shall we start?" Morgan asked.

"Abasi's notebooks mention fragments from the Codex Sinaiticus," Khal said, running his finger along the index and looking for the location.

"I thought that was in the British Library in London?" Morgan said.

Khal looked up, a rueful smile on his face.

"Let's not argue about British imperialistic values, shall we?" he said. "But you're right, the main manuscript is in London. There are fragments here though, kept secret from the researchers by nationalistic monks who thought that at least some of the book should remain here. A previously unseen fragment of the Codex Sinaiticus was discovered in the monastery library in 2009, and we came to research it but more have since been found."

Morgan looked puzzled.

"Why would Abasi be interested in the Codex?" she said. "It's a handwritten copy of the Greek bible, written thousands of years after the supposed Exodus and the period of the Ark."

"True again," Khal said. "But the Codex is one of the most corrected manuscripts in existence as well as the oldest, almost completely preserved copy of the Bible. It is possible that the updates to the document were the result of more ancient books being found, and perhaps the monks also decided that some oral traditions were important enough to change the meaning of words in the Bible."

Morgan nodded. "Go on."

"There are corrections in the book of Exodus that Abasi thought might have clues to the whereabouts of the Ark. We had started to try and unravel it, but the funding ran out and it was considered an unworthy topic of research for scholars in a growing Islamic state. Judaeo-Christian artifacts were of waning interest to the University, but I think it will help us with possible locations."

Morgan watched Khal as he scanned down the list, a crease of concentration between his thick eyebrows. He wore a light chambray striped shirt with elbow patches in darker blue. She smiled a little. He really liked to play the professor, but there weren't too many academics whose rugged features suggested a wild ride bareback on a horse across the desert and whose profile could have been carved on a pharaoh's tomb. He smelled of peppery spices, and her thoughts flickered to some images that would be quite unacceptable in a monastery library.

He looked up at her, sensing her gaze and Morgan quickly looked down at the sheaf of paper in her hands, pretending to look for something interesting.

"The fragment we want is in the archive cases, not the main library shelves," Khal said. "It's this way."

He strode purposefully down the length of the library, the sound of his footsteps dampened by the weight of knowledge that crowded the shelves. Morgan hurried after him as he stopped at a bank of filing cabinets with long, thin drawers. These were the storage areas for manuscript fragments, encased in glass and kept in special conditions to preserve the delicate fabric and skin on which they were written. Khal ran his finger down the tiny labels handwritten in spindly text.

"Here it is." He slid the drawer open. "The monks kept these fragments secret from the researchers because some of them were rightly suspicious of the interest taken in their precious documents. After all, they had looked after them successfully for over a thousand years and then these westerners came suggesting that the fragments needed to be removed for safekeeping."

Morgan bent to the case, inspecting the fragments closely. She was aware of how close she was to Khal and she could feel the warmth of his skin as the hairs on their arms almost touched. She refocused on the text.

"It seems that this fragment was found inside the binding of an eighteenth century book last year," she said, "so it escaped the pillaging of the codex."

Khal smiled. "The monks used the skin in the rebinding of other books, whether to further hide the fragments or just for reuse, no one knows. But certainly there are still pieces missing. In fact, the entire book of Exodus was missing until this fragment came to light, and since then more have been found. You can see where the text has been altered,"

Morgan bent close to the fragment.

"What's it made of?" she asked.

Khal's voice assumed a professorial tone, it was hypnotizing to listen to and she could imagine the adoration of his female students back in his Cairo classroom.

"The Codex was written on prepared animal skin," he said, "made with matching pages from the flesh and hair sides, with flesh sides on the outside of every quire of eight leaves. The pages are easy to tell apart, as the hair pages are darker and absorb ink much better than the flesh side, which is sometimes quite flakey. This design helped with the reconstruction and we also have later texts which enabled the jigsaw puzzle to be put back together."

Morgan nodded. "So we should check the translations of the Exodus verses against the corrected fragments and see whether there are any discrepancies."

She pulled down a couple of Bibles from nearby shelves and they turned their attention to the verses from Exodus, reading through the texts and comparing them to later versions. After a moment, Morgan whispered, "To be honest, my Ancient Greek isn't all that hot anymore."

Khal looked up at her, one dark eyebrow raised. "I wouldn't be so sure about that."

Morgan colored slightly at the suggestion in his eyes. At least she hadn't been imagining the growing attraction between them, but now wasn't the time.

With heads down again, they studied the Exodus verses concerning the Ark. Minutes passed in silence, as both jotted down notes and Morgan found herself happily sinking into the rhythm of research, that rabbit hole of wonder and delight. She had always loved this discovery of ancient knowledge, for there was so much she didn't know, so many things she wanted to learn. This was part of her attraction to ARKANE, their database of knowledge gleaned from mysterious sources around the world and she constantly wanted to plunge into their ocean of ideas.

It was in the deep concentration that came with research that synchronicity would happen, when seemingly unrelated things would crash into each other and hidden meanings emerge. That moment was heady with power, like the release of an energy waiting just beyond consciousness for the point at which we surrender. Morgan surrendered now, waiting for that spark.

After a time, Khal broke the silence.

"There's nothing here that's any different to the translations we know of already, nothing new to suggest where the Ark may be. At least not in these fragments of Exodus."

His words made Morgan wonder aloud. "What about

other books that speak of the Ark, not just the official biblical ones?"

Khal frowned in concentration. "The Codex includes books from the Apocrypha, those not in the official Christian Bible, but still considered important for early church history."

Morgan looked at him. "What about Maccabees?"

"Yes, I believe some books of the Maccabees are in the text. Why?"

"II Maccabees talks about the prophet Jeremiah and where he hid the Ark, so perhaps there's something there."

Khal flicked through the index.

"II Maccabees is missing in the official records, but Abasi must have been here looking for something specific. He had access to the scanned images of the whole text available online, so there must have been something here that gave him further interest. Give me a minute."

Khal walked back down the library to the computer in the records area. Morgan watched him stride away, his frame transforming from academic to desert wanderer as he walked. In just a few minutes, he returned, holding a ledger.

"This contains records of who has been using the library. Abasi was here six weeks ago and he returned with barely contained excitement, but I was off on a dig at the time. I never got the chance to find out what he wanted to tell me about. Perhaps the clue is here." His finger traced down the page. "It says he was looking at a first edition of Homer, dating from the fifteenth century. That's curious, as it's not at all related to our area of research."

"It's worth checking out though," Morgan replied. "Where is it?"

Khal pointed down one of the aisles. "The fifth display case over there."

Morgan pulled on a pair of cotton gloves and went to the

case. Gently she removed the text and in touching the book, she felt a thrill of discovery, for she would have loved to stay and drink in the words on these pages, this other world of ancient Greece. She opened the cover and carefully turned the pages.

"There, what's that?" As he spoke, Khal reached out and took her hand. His fingers felt hot on her skin and Morgan registered that he held her for just a second too long. "It looks like a manuscript fragment."

Morgan teased the fragment delicately from the pages of the book and laid it on the glass case.

"It looks just like the other Codex fragments, but what is it doing in here?" she said.

"Maybe Abasi hid it here. There must be something important in it. Let's try comparing the texts again."

Khal held open the Septuagint translation of the Bible, which contained the Apocryphal books including II Maccabees. He found the specific verse and took it over to where Morgan had laid out the glass panel with the fragment. He set the book down gently. Together they worked on the passage, noting potential translation issues with the words. Morgan moved her head back and forth between the texts, trying to see the difference. Then she saw it.

"It's the mountain," she said.

Khal straightened and rubbed his neck. "What do you mean?"

Morgan spoke in a whisper, aware that what they had found was potentially explosive.

"Look. In the Septuagint translation that everyone uses, it says that Jeremiah went away to the mountain *from the top of which* Moses saw God's Promised Land. When he reached the mountain, Jeremiah found a cave dwelling; he carried the tent, the ark, and the incense altar into it, then blocked up the entrance. So this suggests that it was on the mountain where Moses saw the promised land."

Khal nodded. "It's known as Mount Nebo in Jordan, but it has been searched from top to bottom. American fundamentalists have even used ground penetrating radar to try to find it and the Ark's not there."

"But look at this difference." Morgan pointed to the page. "The fragment actually says that Jeremiah went away to the mountain from the top of which *he could see where* Moses saw God's Promised Land. Which means he could see Mount Nebo from where he stood, but he wasn't actually on Mount Nebo."

Khal looked stunned. "So the later version has been changed, and just that one phrase changes the geographic possibilities entirely."

Morgan nodded.

"I'll get this back to Martin at ARKANE," she said, "and have him work on alternative locations, but we need to head to Jordan. If we start driving now, we can make it by lunchtime tomorrow."

Khal turned to return the book to the case as Morgan started to walk back down the library corridor. Two monks stepped out from behind one of the large bookcases. With their habits touching the floor and cowls pulled over their faces, it was as if they glided into place in the middle of the corridor. They stood silently, blocking Morgan's path. She tensed, feeling a threat, but she was also puzzled, since they were in such a holy place and a threat seemed incongruous.

"Good morning, brothers," she said, first in Arabic and then in English. There was no response. Khal tried to justify their presence.

"The Abbot has allowed us this access to examine papers in this case," he said. "And we are just leaving."

The two men stepped forward, but Morgan still couldn't see their faces. She felt an adrenalin rush and welcomed it, for her Krav Maga skills had been useful for the ARKANE missions so far. She didn't know how Khal would react to violence here, but she could see no choice. Of course, the best defense would be to run, but that didn't seem to be an option, so offense was the next best thing.

She yelled at them, the roar of a lioness readying for battle erupting from her throat. It should have brought others running but it only triggered the men into action. They rushed forward, one at Morgan and the other at Khal. Morgan saw the flash of a blade as the monk attacked and she held her ground until the last moment, feeling behind her for one of the heavy books.

As he swung his arm, she pulled the book in front of her. The knife thudded into the Greek Bible as she sidestepped and used his momentum to carry him further forward, smashing the heel of her palm into the monk's face as he passed. There was a satisfying crunch as she connected with his nose, his hood flew back and blood dripped down his face. He shook his head to clear his vision as out of the corner of her eye Morgan saw Khal on the floor, using his legs to try and kick the other monk away. She knew that the assassin was toying with his prey for the academic was no match for a trained fighter.

Morgan launched herself at her attacker, striking his ear with a hammer fist, following through with an elbow to his chin. The man spun round and crashed to the floor. The other monk saw what was happening and left Khal to run towards her, feinting with his knife. As he lunged, Morgan turned to one side, grabbing his wrists and pulling him forward and down. She jerked her knee up and it connected with his face, then she used all of her body weight to bring an elbow down on the back of his neck. He fell heavily, unconscious.

The first man was groaning so she turned and booted him in the head. It was as if the rage she had been bottling up over Jake had exploded, and now these men would pay the price. She felt the throbbing in her side intensify, but the pain only helped her focus, and she soared on the edge of oblivion. Her surroundings faded away and she only saw only a manifestation of hatred and danger as she kicked at the prone bodies. She would make sure these men didn't get up again.

"Morgan!" Khal's voice pierced the haze. "Morgan, I think they're done."

She turned, hands raised in Krav Maga open stance, ready to strike again. He saw the violence in her eyes and backed off.

"It's OK now," he said, voice tentative, as if expecting her to strike him. "We should leave because there may be more of them. You can clearly handle it, but I'd rather run."

Morgan's head began to clear as one of the men on the floor coughed and moaned. She kicked him again and he sank back to the floor. Khal looked at her and she shrugged.

"You don't want them following us, do you?" she said. "OK, let's get out of here. We know where we need to go."

As the library door closed behind them, one of the injured monks slowly sat up, fumbling for the cell phone deep within the folds of his robe. Wiping blood from his eyes, he tapped out a message and hit Send. Al-Hirbaa would pay handsomely for this information and the bitch who had beaten them would get her violent reward.

En route to Jordan. 8.14pm

The last of the sun disappeared beyond the Sinai horizon and Khal watched the shadows lengthen into chill night. With one hand on the wheel, he pulled his jacket on and then leaned over to pull Morgan's coat further up so it covered her sleeping form. They had rushed out of the monastery compound earlier, not stopping to speak to the Abbot for fear of further attacks. Morgan had said little as they grabbed their bags and headed out to the vehicle. Once they had set off, she had fallen asleep, the after effects of the fight surely exhausting her. Khal glanced over at her sleeping form. She clearly had military training and could handle herself, but he wondered how far she would have gone if he hadn't stopped her. There was clearly a current of rage under her usually calm exterior.

Khal was comfortable driving this route and he relaxed into the road. He had done his military service fifteen years ago and drove this desert road on patrol. The Arab Spring had brought renewed tension, including violence at the border crossing with Israel and a mob attack on the Israeli embassy in Cairo, but Egypt depended on the tourist trade and had to encourage foreigners. The route from Sinai to Israel and up into Jordan was a regular route for pilgrim tourists who wanted to visit holy sites as well as Petra. There were a few night buses and taxis on the road, but otherwise the hours passed in darkness and peace, the only sound the whistling of the wind through the window. Khal had wound it down fully so that he could smell the night air and feel it, cool on his skin.

He finally had time to think after the crazy few days they had just been through. He didn't know how Morgan managed to stay so calm. He wanted to help her, but he also felt that his place was at the university or the dig, while this was a little beyond his capabilities. But Morgan had brought a ray of light into his life, cutting through the dry routine he had created for himself, and giving him a glimpse of something he had missed for so long.

His thoughts went to Meena and the days they had had together, before a fast-growing tumor had ravaged his wife's body and left her a shell. In the days before she died, she had asked him to live well and find a new wife, someone who would give him sons and love him as she had. But after her death, he had thrown himself into work, ignoring the flirtatious looks of the girls on the summer digs. Abasi had gently chided him, trying to get him to go to university parties and social events, but Khal had only found solace in work. Morgan was very different to Meena, but it was the first time he had felt real desire in a long time. He glanced over at her profile. She was frowning in her sleep, her lips faintly moving. It seemed that demons haunted them both.

It was only a few hours' drive to Nuweiba, a coastal town from which they could get a ferry to Jordan in order to avoid the Israeli border crossing.

"Are we nearly there yet?" Morgan's whisper came in the dark.

Khal laughed softly, not wanting to break the spell of night. "Maybe thirty minutes more to Nuweiba."

Morgan put her seat back up and rubbed her eyes. "Are you okay with all this driving?"

"I'm fine," he said. "You can have the crazy Jordanian side while I get some sleep. Are you sure we'll be able to get a ferry at this time of night?"

Morgan nodded. "American dollars speak louder than ferry timetables."

They reached Nuweiba around midnight, passing tourists in the resort town lying on couches near the beach, smoking sheesha pipes and drinking lurid cocktails. The tourist trade had lessened with the political situation, so any who made it this far were taking advantage of the good times, before the hordes realized it was safe to return.

"Fancy a bit of espionage?" she asked Khal, as they climbed out of the car and stretched their aching limbs. "Perhaps you'd like to do the honors?"

She pushed a roll of dollars into his hand, her fingers wrapping around his as she stepped close. He felt a wave of panic rise, and then subside as he realized that there would be no violence here, just a negotiation, and he was Egyptian after all. He could probably get a better deal than Morgan ever could as a female Westerner. He took the money and approached the jetty. There were large ferries but also fast catamarans for hire and Khal spotted one that would do nicely, where the skipper was playing cards on the deck. Waving him over, Khal negotiated a price and then beckoned for Morgan to jump on as he handed her the change.

"Hm, that's a good rate," she said, smiling up at him. "I'll need to take you on some more adventures."

Khal smiled as he gave her a hand up into the boat, and felt stupidly pleased with himself. But he felt a sense of trepidation at the next step of the journey to Jordan, for what if they really did find the Ark?

CHAPTER 12

City of the Dead, Cairo, Egypt. 11.48pm

THE TAXI CRAWLED THROUGH the tight, weaving streets, the driver honking at donkeys and pedestrians to get out of his way. After the long journey back from Zimbabwe, Natasha was tired, but she needed to make better progress in the search for the Ark and she was at a dead end. The notebook had pointed in two directions and belatedly it seemed that Sinai was the right one after all.

She had received a text message and a longer email from al-Hirbaa, informing her that the late curator's assistant had been spotted in Sinai. It seemed he had help from the ARKANE agent, Morgan Sierra. Natasha felt a wave of anger, because the bitch had tricked her. Sierra should have died that night in the Sedlec bone church. Natasha blamed her for the loss of Milan Noble but she also wanted to find the Ark. Perhaps following the academics would achieve the goal faster.

Tonight she needed to connect again, to make herself right with the gods and her ancestors. Then she would be able to move on tomorrow in the sure knowledge that the Divine was on her side. Here in Cairo's necropolis she would summon their spirits to aid her. She had neglected the ancient ways while in Europe, although she had made blood sacrifices to another cause. Now she knew that she must approach the gods on bended knee, before the shade of her father, and summon their help in the search for the Ark.

The City of the Dead was not a necropolis in the European sense, but more like a Roman town where the tombs were like small houses. Families had squatted amongst the tombs since the Cairo earthquake of 1992, forgotten refugees isolated in their own city. Some were here to be closer to their ancestors, but most were dispossessed, forced from Cairo as it had grown into a mega-city.

The poorest lived in the slum of Manshiyat Naser, the Garbage City, and there children worked in the steaming heaps of rubbish, eking out an existence on the edge of violence and certain early death. It was there that Isac had gone tonight to find a suitable sacrifice, for even if the people noticed a disappearance, nobody cared enough to investigate. They were beneath the rights of any law, existing in a no man's land, neither living nor dead. Natasha watched the ragged people gaze listlessly at the taxi as it passed. It seemed to her that they were ghosts, living on the edge of death, and she saw only a waste of life in their eyes.

Finally, the taxi reached the tomb of the El-Beherys, which lay in one of the oldest parts of the cemetery. The area was mostly pedestrianized, so narrow were the streets. Natasha stepped out of the taxi a block away, pulling her robes more tightly around her face, for she didn't want to be recognized. Hurrying along the street towards the tomb, she saw the guard sitting by the doorway. He stood as soon as she drew near, alert for any danger, and she pulled her shawl from her face so he could identify her.

"Are the others here yet?" she asked as he acknowledged her.

The guard shook his head. "You're the first."

His eyes lowered as he spoke, as he knew the reputation of the El-Beherys. For the sake of his children, he kept his eyes averted and his ears closed. This job was mostly tedious but when the tomb was used, it was a night of evil he tried desperately to purge from his memory. Some who entered this tomb never emerged, and he had seen the blood that had to be cleaned the next day. He turned and unlocked the heavy door, pushing it open so Natasha could enter. She swept in and he closed the door behind her.

Natasha took a pen torch from her bag, clicked it on and then lit the thick candles that sat in the corners of the stone mausoleum, built for generations of El-Beherys and added to over time. Embalmed bodies were laid in alcoves around the walls. An altar sat in the middle of the space, channels cut into the stone below it that angled down towards a drain at the back of the mausoleum. At each corner of the altar, leather straps hung down, worn from years of use, and there was an earthy smell in the air as if the place was alive and fecund.

Natasha went to one of the alcoves and greeted the body of her father, mummified according to their tradition. Her family believed that the Ba, or spirit, remained in the tomb and could still act in the physical world. In her rational moments, Natasha doubted this, but here in the crypt, she felt the presence of her ancestors and as she touched her lips to the forehead of the mummy, she thought back to her memories of the man who had guided her life.

Born when he turned 50, she was the last of his sixteen children, his little princess. She was also the one most interested in ancient Egypt, so he doted on her and took her out of school to archaeological digs, letting her wear jewelry he took from the tombs. Her mother had been a beautiful Russian immigrant taken as a wife in the heat of lust and cast off as soon as the baby was born, so Natasha was raised by his other wives.

At seven years old she had started killing animals and birds in the garden, staking them out in the sun and stabbing them with the ritual knife her father had given her. She made the other children watch and they cried, but her father just laughed, swinging her up above his head, making her squeal with laughter. Then one day he had hit her for the first time. Without hesitation, she had bitten his hand and scratched at him. He praised her spirit and from that day, had started to train her to hit back properly, and then to become the aggressor.

"You are my little warrior princess," he would say. "And I shall make you queen one day."

When she was thirteen Natasha took to cutting herself, the sight of blood exciting her, the pain just on the edge of pleasure. She made sure to hide the scars until one day her father noticed. She forced a tear from her eye and pointed at one of the wives. He turned in rage and backhanded his wife, sending her flying across the floor.

Natasha watched as he punched her face and then kicked her in the ribs, his boot making a thumping noise. The woman groaned, blood trickling from her mouth to the dusty ground. Her father called for his guards and they threw the woman out onto the streets. He had gathered her in his arms, saying, "No one hurts my little princess."

Her position in the household changed after that. The other wives and children were respectful, afraid and kept their distance, eyes averted from her torture of animals and birds. Natasha grew into a beautiful young woman, with deep dark eyes and slender curves. She saw her father's eyes grow hungry when he looked at her and then darken with fear and regret. She recognized a new kind of power and would lean against him, her young breasts pushed against his arm. He would shift but she would cling to him, pulling herself onto his lap.

"Papa, perhaps I could come with you to the meeting tonight?" she asked one evening, squirming a little on his lap as if she was trying to get comfortable, but with the bulge in his pants, she could tell he was aroused by her proximity.

"It's too old for you, my darling. It's not for children."

"I'm no longer a child, Papa, you must see that. I want to be your princess at the temple."

She had watched as his Adam's apple bobbed and he swallowed. His eyes closed as he gave into forbidden sensations.

"Then you must trust me and do as I say," he said huskily. "It will be difficult, but if you make it through the rituals, then you will be part of the ancient line that stretches back to the pharaohs." That night, she had honored him and other men with her body and many nights after that. Tonight she would honor him again and the Gods would reward her with the triumph of the Ark.

Natasha walked the length of the tomb and greeted all of her ancestors, asking for their blessing on the rituals she would soon perform. She remembered first coming here, mute with fear, watching as her father carved a man into pieces and then held them up to the gods. It was a ritual to mimic the dismemberment of Osiris at the hands of his brother, Seth, after which Isis had collected the parts to remake his body. She had made Osiris a new penis and become pregnant in the few precious moments during which he had breathed again before sinking back into darkness, ruler of the Duat, the eternal kingdom of death.

Her father had made Natasha hold a piece of the body that night and warm blood had dripped down her arms. The smell made her retch and gag, but her father's eyes held her motionless, for he would not countenance weakness in his daughter. The next time, he had made her cut until she eventually began to see human flesh as mere meat.

Natasha opened a large chest, its workings well oiled. She reverently unwrapped the ritual masks and laid them next to the altar. She ran her fingers over the Horus mask, caressing the feathers of the falcon who soared above the earth, god of the sky who rose above mere mortal life. She would call on him, but tonight she would be Isis incarnate.

A knock came at the door and Isac was admitted. Behind him two other men dragged a bound and gagged youth who struggled against his bonds.

"Apologies for our late-coming," Isac said. "This one was hard to subdue, but the gods will be pleased with such a strong sacrifice."

Natasha walked over to the young man. He had lithe muscles from manual labor and skin the color of burnt caramel. His eyes were wild with fear and anger above the tight gag, but she could see that he was intrigued to see her there. No doubt he was thinking that he would be safe with a woman present. He wore a rough shirt, faded through washing and many days under the sun. She unbuttoned it as the other men held him tight, his muscles straining against their bondage.

"I like a bit of spirit," she said as she stroked his taut stomach with her fingertips. "Are you ready to perform for the gods?"

The young man was clearly aroused and yet puzzled by what was going on. Natasha slid her hand down further to caress his hardness and he groaned through the tight gag, turning his head away.

"Wait a little," she whispered to him. She turned to Isac. "Prepare the ritual."

The men pushed the young man onto the altar and fastened the four straps to his limbs. He struggled, but the bonds held tight.

Isac and the others put on the masks of Horus, Anubis, the jackal, and Thoth, the baboon-headed god. Natasha pulled off her outer robe to reveal a white sheath dress that wrapped tightly around her body. She picked up the tall head-dress of Isis and placed it on her head. At that moment, she felt transformed into Isis, protector of the dead, worshipped as the mother goddess as well as the ruler of magic and nature.

Her father had understood the power of the goddess and his own wives had failed to bring him honor by taking the role, so he had schooled Natasha to perform the rites. Isac had accompanied her for many of the years they had done this and tonight they would take the rites to the final sacrifice together.

Natasha stood at the head of the altar and the other three stood at the sides, so four of them surrounded the bound youth, still struggling and groaning through his gag.

"The chalice," Natasha commanded.

Isac, as Horus, stepped forward and gave her a large copper bowl filled with what looked like muddy water. She drank a long draft and relaxed as the hallucinogen began to work on her. First her lips went numb, then she felt her heart race. The candlelight merged with the stone walls and spirits began to leak from the tombs with the faces of her ancestors, their lips begging her to begin the bloody rite.

As she succumbed to the pull of the drug, Natasha found a strange symmetry in her quest. For some claimed that the manna eaten by the Israelites in the desert of the Exodus journey was a bread containing ergot, a fungus with the same psychoactive base chemicals as LSD, similar to that which they now imbibed. The bowl was filled again and each of the men drank. Before Isac took his own draught, he lowered the gag and poured the liquid into the throat of the tied man, holding his nose so he was forced to drink, before raising the gag again.

Now came the part Natasha loved most, when the curtain between the real world and the spirit realm was torn down and she could see into the void between them. Her body became a vessel for the goddess and these men the witnesses to the eternal struggle between life and death. At this point she thought nothing of the Ark quest, for her physical self was just a shell, an outer form.

She watched the figures of the men as they twisted into

therianthropic forms, their animal heads becoming visages of the divine, the pantheon she worshipped and of which she was now part. Her body was touched all over with fire, as her skin became super-sensitive. Her mind started to whirl, as shadows in the tomb morphed into djinns that reached out to her, misshapen mouths open, calling out, their tongues lapping at her skin. Flashbacks of her father came to her in this state, how her pain had become his pleasure and her sacrifice made him proud enough to call her daughter, the favorite one.

"Tonight you will be Osiris, tonight you will see the gods in the afterlife," Natasha said, beginning the chants of the ancient rite. Her voice mingled with Isac's in the chorus and she felt the rise of power within. She moved to the side of the altar and touched the bound man intimately, calling on the Gods to see her act in uniting heaven with earth. Isac helped her to mount him and she began to ride the man, feeling him hard inside her as the drugs spiraled her up into the heavens with pleasure.

"I call on Seth, god of chaos and storms," she prayed, as she undulated her hips, teasing out the sexual tension, feeling the eyes of the men on her. "Hear my plea and send me what I need to complete the quest. This is for you."

Natasha felt the ritual knife in her hand as she neared her own peak, plunging down onto him as the young man groaned his release and she squeezed him deep inside her. Leaning forward, she thrust the knife up under his ribs, then pulled it from him as blood welled up, staining her dress. She stabbed it down into his chest again and again as she called to heaven. The young man's eyes were wide with fear and agony and she felt him shrink within her as she called out to the gods to see her sacrifice and reward her with victory.

She watched the life leave his eyes and felt his spirit rise from his corpse to join the others that swirled around her in the room. The gods were here and she reveled in their touch as she slid from the altar and began the bloody business of hacking up the corpse, the other men joining her to finish the sacrifice.

Much later, Natasha felt the cold of the ground permeate her clothes as she lay on the floor of the tomb. The stink of blood and sex mingled with death and decay hung in the air. The after-effects of the drug meant she had to choke back vomit that threatened to erupt from her. She despised the new life within her, for it made her physically weak and brought her low. She would get rid of it, as soon as the Ark was delivered to Jerusalem.

Natasha struggled up onto her hands and knees, then hauled herself up one of the pillars. The slashed limbs of the dead boy were limp on the altar, his head had rolled to one side with eyes open, his blood congealed in pools across the floor. She was covered with gore, as were the men who lay curled on the floor, sated from the violent frenzy. She never knew which of them she had sex with after the ritual, for it just became a haze of blood lust and the high of drugs mixed with sexual ecstasy. This too honored the gods, and they would reward her sacrifice.

Isac began to stir as Natasha pulled her bag from behind one of the mummified bodies and withdrew her cloak. She wrapped it around herself to hide her bloody clothes and then felt in the pocket. She pulled out her smartphone and saw a number of messages from al-Hirbaa. She opened the first and smiled, for the Gods had already rewarded her faithfulness. They needed to head for Jordan.

DAY 5

CHAPTER 13

Nuweiba to Aqaba, Jordan. 4.07am

MORGAN GAZED OUT AT the inky blackness of the Red Sea, her thoughts lulled by the slap of waves on the hull. It was as if time had been suspended and she could be still in the dark, all the rushing around put on hold for this period of calm before the next storm. Khal was sleeping in one of the cabins, tired after the long drive, but Morgan needed some time to think, so here she was, looking out to sea.

The black of night camouflaged the turquoise waters beneath which she had scuba dived so many times. Just to the north was Eilat, the Israeli resort town where during the day girls in bikinis lay on the beach and muscled boys showed off their volleyball skills. She smiled softly at the memories of how she and Elian had spent holidays there with their IDF friends. Young bodies idle in the sun, covered in sand, his arm thrown across her in sleep.

When Elian had died, shot to pieces on the Golan Heights, she had retreated from that kind of fun, as it seemed irreverent somehow. His body was cold in the tomb so how could she be laughing in the sun? She had thrown herself into her work, research on understanding fundamentalism. Only by eradicating it on all sides could there be peace between Jews and Arabs. Her passion had driven a wedge between her and her old friends, who thought she was trying to help create a solution that was a fantasy.

Now Morgan was back looking for the Ark, an artifact that could bring instant conflict to her home, or perhaps bring some kind of salvation. She shivered in the night breeze, for the Scriptures showed the Ark to be a weapon, a thing of terror and power that could strike down enemies with bolts of thunder. She knew of those within the Israeli Defense Force who would dearly love to get their hands on such a thing, divinely fashioned for the people chosen by God himself. Regardless of how she felt about the religious and political implications, it would be better if ARKANE held the Ark and not one of the parties in the Middle East. For even those who were as doves might prove to be hawks once they had their hands on something potentially explosive.

The boat neared the shore and night faded as the lights of the port of Aqaba grew brighter. Morgan turned from Eilat towards Jordan's only port, bustling with people scurrying over cargo ships at this early hour. Man-made industry was surrounded by the russet mountains of the Jordanian interior, perched on the edge of a primal land that looked like it could easily shrug off this insignificant intruder. Giant cargo ships loomed over the little ferry as it navigated the docks, just as Khal emerged from the cabin, holding two mugs of coffee.

"It's not great, but it might keep us going for a bit," he said.

Morgan smiled and took it from him, their fingers brushing and she saw the way he looked at her. For a moment she thought that an arm around her, a strong shoulder to lean into, would help more than the caffeine. He looked even more like a rugged movie star after a rough night's travel, the dark stubble on his chin sculpting his jawline. The thought of how it would feel on her skin flitted across her mind and she turned away quickly. Khal sat next to her watching the progress of the ferry into port.

They finished their coffee as the boat docked and then they slipped off towards the customs house. It seemed appropriate, Morgan thought, that they were two travelers in search of the ancient Ark entering through a trade route that had been inhabited since 4000BC. Aqaba, the biblical Edom, had become the kingdom of the Nabateans and then, in the first century AD, it was one of the main Roman ports in the area, later passed down through the hands of the Islamic dynasties. In modern history, Aqaba had been the site of a battle in World War I won by the British. Now it was a fast growing port and resort town with watersports vying with the giant boats for domination of the coral-filled waters.

Morgan and Khal headed for a line of taxis and car hire booths where men sat in the early morning drinking coffee and smoking Polo cigarettes. Khal negotiated a rate for the next few days of hire and they were led to a car park dominated by incongruous Japanese cars. Morgan laughed as they got in, throwing the little baggage they had in the back.

"International antiquities hunting in a Toyota Yaris," she said. "Don't say I never show you a good time!"

CHAPTER 14

Petra, Jordan, 7.18am

EVEN THOUGH IT WAS still early, the sun beat down as Morgan and Khal pulled into the car park at Petra, the ancient capital of the Nabateans, established in the sixth century BC. The main tourist buses arrived much later so the place was still quiet. Local men were opening up their shops and drinking coffee in patches of sun, preparing for the daily onslaught of tourists. Dusty camels with saddles in muted colors sat on the ground, chewing, their legs folded under them. Horses and donkeys stamped in the corners of the square, ready to be ridden by tourists who didn't want to walk the kilometers around the city.

Morgan opened the door of the hire car, bracing herself for the heat.

"We need a break. Let's explore before the rest of the tourists get here. Are your negotiation muscles up for some more flexing this morning?"

Khal smiled, saying nothing, but headed off towards the ticket office with a purposeful stride. Morgan watched him walk. He was confident, for he knew archaeology, and his academic skills could shine here. Morgan felt calm with Khal, for he didn't have that latent physical energy that Jake seemed to exude, always moving and restless. Khal was self-contained, his deeper thoughts protected by a wall of academic professionalism.

After a moment, she saw him wave triumphantly from the ticket booth, his baksheesh accepted as an early morning bonus. Together they walked into the Siq, a narrow gorge in the red sandstone that led to the city carved out of rock. The sky was cobalt blue over their heads between the walls that stretched high towards the heavens, the colors muted this early in the day and the air cooler in the sheltered gorge. The cry of desert birds echoed off the walls, the only sound apart from their footsteps. It was an eerie place to be with no people, as if the ghosts of the Nabateans still remained, their souls trapped by the constant reanimation of the place, sucking the energy from tourists who tramped the beaten paths.

Petra was a fortress city, defended by its location deep in the rock canyons and watered by a perennial stream. In the fourth century AD, an earthquake had brought destruction, and under the Romans, the city went into decline. Later, the ruins had been ransacked and Morgan felt a sense of hubris here, the pride and arrogance of kings who thought their age would last forever, just before the gods brought them low. This lesson was repeated in every empire, with great men believing that the sun would never set on their power, only to find the inevitable end just around the corner. Morgan was grateful for Khal's silent introspection, and they were comfortable as they walked in the silence, both thinking their own thoughts.

They rounded a corner in the Siq and there it was, Al-Khazneh, the Treasury. With a massive facade carved into the rock face, the classical temple was actually the tomb of a Nabatean King.

"A rose-red city half as old as time," Morgan whispered as she looked towards the ruins.

"Eternal, silent, beautiful, alone." Khal responded.

Morgan turned to find his eyes on her as he spoke the poetry of John William Burgon, a paean to the city. Khal was full of surprises, she thought, and the tension between them was taut, stretching for a long moment. Khal broke it by pulling off his backpack.

"Coffee?" he asked, producing a flask.

Morgan grinned. "You're a saint. Where did you get this?"

"I bought it from the car hire guy. He totally ripped me off but I thought it would be worth it, and I have pita and labneh."

Morgan's stomach rumbled on cue. She loved the soft cheese, and being looked after in this way was something new. Feeding someone was an important sign of hospitality, necessary for guests in the Middle East. Khal was a true son of these parts, but she had become more English now, forgetting the ways of her homeland.

A finger of sunlight lit a patch of red earth in the middle of the open ground in front of the Treasury, so they sat and Khal filled the thermos cup with steaming black coffee. He passed it to Morgan and she took a sip to test the temperature before taking a deep draught of the hot black liquid.

"Just how I like it," Morgan said. She knew she was a caffeine addict, but it was pretty much her only vice and everybody needed something to indulge in, she thought. She gave the cup to Khal and he refilled it before taking a sip.

"We could just stay here," he said. "It's like nothing exists but this place, this moment."

Morgan sighed.

"Yes, but as soon as the tourists arrive, the peace will be shattered and the clock will still be ticking towards the President's arrival in Jerusalem." She smiled at him. "But we can at least enjoy our coffee break."

Morgan looked up at the rocks around her. Staircases were cut into the sheer face, many leading nowhere, as if the stonecutters had been aiming for the gods and fallen to their deaths before they could finish their journey.

"Did you know that Petra has links to the Exodus story?" Khal offered another cup of coffee with his knowledge. Morgan accepted both. "This is Wadi Musa, and according to Arab tradition, Moses struck his staff here and water sprang from the earth for the Israelites to drink. Moses' brother Aaron is buried near here on the mountain named for him."

Morgan crumbled some of the red earth between her fingers.

"That's why I love this part of the world," she said. "Every rock has a history, every town a story that goes back millennia. Sometimes the veil of time is torn back and you can see what the past was like, but then the modern world intrudes and the illusion is shattered. Israel has such an intensity of both, moments of glory and then times where you lament that it was ever born, for troubles lie so deep in the country."

Khal looked at her and Morgan felt he could read her soul.

"You love it though, your Israel," he said. "I can see that. No matter how hard you try to escape it."

Morgan sighed. "It's not the country of my birth, but I feel it in my blood. Just being here in this landscape reminds me of the Jordan Valley, the Dead Sea, the cliffs of Masada. It's like coming home, yet I'm torn now, between my new life and my old."

Khal nodded with understanding.

"That feeling will never leave you. I know it well for I am sometimes in love with my country and its great history, then frustrated at the craziness of what it has become. Our national identity is schizophrenic, the tombs of the pharaohs versus the Arab Spring and nascent Islamic fundamentalists. This is a time of great change, Morgan, but we can't deny our love for the countries that call us."

Khal reached for her hand and squeezed it.

"My father loved it here," Morgan said. "He used to take me for walks in the hills of Galilee and tell me stories of the digs there. He never treated me like a child, more as an equal, so he didn't spare the gory details. I remember once at Tell Megiddo, the biblical Armageddon, he told me of the 26 layers of ruins that lay beneath us. Each version of the city was razed to the ground, and all the slaughtered citizens lay under our feet, the bones of generations. I had nightmares for weeks."

"It sounds like a fascinating childhood," Khal said, "I'm jealous, for my youth was not so idyllic."

Morgan turned to him, "Really?"

"I was born in Ezbet El Nakhi, the slum of Cairo," Khal said, "and by aged five I was sorting rubbish from the tips. I should have died there but somehow a Christian mission found me and began my education. My mother was too pleased to protest that her Muslim son was going to a Christian school, especially as she barely found enough food for the other children. She died when I was seven and I moved into a mission school. They fed my love of ancient Egypt and my desire to help reconcile the faiths in my country, and they supported me in my studies."

Morgan touched Khal's arm, seeing the pain in his eyes. "So why the regrets?"

"Although I gained a new family and a new life, I lost touch with my brothers and sister, who were swallowed up by the rubbish tips of Ezbet. They could be anywhere now, perhaps even martyrs for the fundamentalist cause, since they recruit from the ranks of the hopeless. I looked for them, and sometimes I still think I see one of them in the street ..." Khal paused and held up his coffee cup. "But enough of my melancholy. Here's to the success of opposites, the triumph of archaeology over politics."

Morgan laughed. "Cheers."

Khal took a long swig and then passed it back to Morgan. Finishing the cup, she stood, brushing the red dust from where it clung to her slender form.

"I will not have my city torn apart, Khal. Two of the most glorious landmarks blown apart by extremists? Not on my watch. Let's find us an Ark."

CHAPTER 15

Mount Nebo, Jordan, 12.38pm

THE JORDANIAN LANDSCAPE WAS hypnotic in its repetition but the hours passed steadily as Morgan and Khal drove north. The blue of the sky blended with earth the color of ground bones and dark green scrub trees dotted the landscape. Birds of prey hovered in the heat waves above them, keen eyes searching for rodents that scurried between holes and lizards that darted under rocks.

Finally, Morgan pulled into the car park at Mount Nebo. Groves of cedar and pine broke up the monotony of the rocky ground here, as the mountain stepped down towards the plateau. The summit was busy with coaches, and groups of tourists in matching baseball caps stood surveying the landscape under a burning sun. They looked out at a wide expanse, trying to catch a glimpse of the shores of the Dead Sea and the cities of Jericho and Jerusalem in the misty distance. The cities were sometimes visible on a clear day but today the haze shrouded them.

Morgan and Khal got out of the car and stretched. Morgan rolled her shoulders as she heard the nearest tour guide talking to a group of Christians.

"This is where God showed Moses the land of Canaan. You might call it 'the Promised Land,' but in Jordan, you can't say that for political reasons, so we'll just call it the land of Canaan."

Morgan smiled. The knife edge of tourist dollars, religion and political correctness was always sharp here in the Middle East. Khal walked around the car to stand next to her.

"Please tell me we don't have to listen to this stuff?" he whispered.

She smiled. "Are you sure? It might be fascinating."

Khal raised an eyebrow. "You can give me the potted version."

They grabbed their backpacks and Morgan led the way, down the road away from the summit towards the nearby foothills which had a view back to the famous Mount. Morgan pulled her smartphone from her pocket and opened the ARKANE GPS app.

"Martin Klein, the analyst at ARKANE, has sent me the location of a cave system on the east side of the mountain that we're going to examine first," she said. "It fits the description in II Maccabees. Apparently Jeremiah's followers came to look for the Ark immediately after it had been hidden but they couldn't find it. Jeremiah reprimanded them, saying that it would be hidden until God gathered his people at the end times, when the glory of the Lord would appear again."

"But the Jeremiah tradition is little known," Khal said, "at least amongst the conspiracy theorists who still think that the Ark is in Ethiopia, and the fundamental Christians who consider the Apocrypha to be heresy." His strides easily matched Morgan's pace as they hurried down the mountain.

"Exactly," Morgan replied. "There's something else I've been thinking about as well. Do you know about the Copper Scroll?"

"One of the Dead Sea scrolls? The one with all the treasure?"

Morgan nodded.

"Exactly. The Copper Scroll was found near Qumran, pretty close to where we are. It lists 64 underground hiding places where treasure had been hidden. It's considered to be a priestly document from Jerusalem, but the locations can't be tied specifically to places as they are in a kind of code that, as yet, no one has cracked."

"You think it refers to the Ark?" Khal asked.

"It talks about the tabernacle and golden fixtures hidden in an opening under the ascent, on a mountain facing eastwards, covered by forty placed boulders. Together with the verse from Maccabees, it may refer to the Ark. It's worth a try anyway." Morgan paused, looking at the app on her phone. "We need to head north here."

She led Khal off the road and onto the dusty rock-strewn ground. The trees were thicker here so they had some shade, nevertheless, Morgan felt the sweat run down her back from the heat of the midday sun. Looking down at the smartphone, she followed the tiny arrow across the hillside. She tripped suddenly, stubbing her toe on a large rock. Khal reached out to steady her, his fingers strong on her arm.

"Careful now," he said, his eyes showing concern. "I need you in one piece."

His words echoed through Morgan's brain as he looked away quickly, realizing he might have said too much. He walked on ahead of her and she watched him, acutely aware of the electricity in their touch. He turned back, his body tense.

"We've found the caves, but they're down there." Khal pointed over a sharp escarpment and Morgan looked over down to where he pointed.

"The contours of the mountain weren't shown on the map," she said, "so we'll have to go around first and then down."

They started to walk down the edge of the steep slope, chunks of rock skimming into the air as their boots trod deep into the dusty earth. Walking on this land reminded Morgan of her military service in Israel, tramping on patrol, the sound of helicopters overhead. She stopped and Khal halted, waiting for her as she realized that she wasn't just daydreaming. The noise of helicopters was not in her memory. It was real.

"I hear them," Khal said, cocking his head to one side. "Maybe two."

"Not Israeli, not here," Morgan said. "They must be Jordanian so maybe they're not coming here."

But she felt a prickle of fear and set off faster down the slope, almost jogging, as Khal strode by her side, both of them aware of how vulnerable they were on this open terrain. They needed cover quickly and the caves were their only option.

The escarpment became a gentler slope and as soon as they could safely run, Morgan and Khal jogged across the rocky ground to the opening of the caves. They could see two helicopters approaching now, flying low and heading directly for Mount Nebo. There were three larger cave entrances and a smaller one, so Morgan ducked into the first large cave entrance, her breathing fast from the exertion. She was still not completely recovered from her injuries but Khal had barely broken a sweat. He was certainly fit for an archaeologist, Morgan thought.

"Do you think they're coming to these caves?" he said, his voice concerned.

"Perhaps they'll just pass over, but we need to find somewhere to hide just in case, and we might as well search the caves while we look."

Morgan pulled a torch from her backpack and walked deeper into the cave as Khal followed. The sound of helicopters grew closer and louder, and then the rotors whined to a halt close by. Morgan crept back to the entrance.

"They've landed just down the slope," she whispered,

checking the smartphone. There was no reception, so she couldn't even signal to ARKANE for backup, even if they could make it in time. She and Khal carried no weapons, little money and they had no negotiating power, but then Morgan hadn't been expecting company. She peered around the cave entrance and saw four figures emerging from the first helicopter, and three more from the second.

"Those are military utility helicopters," she said, recognizing the Hughes MD500 series. "They didn't bring the Cobra attack choppers so this is a civilian group escorted by military and I don't expect they'd be looking for engagement." Khal seemed to relax a little. Being taken into custody by any Middle Eastern military service was never going to be a pleasant experience. Morgan had the backing of the British government, but he had nothing. "But they are coming up the slope towards the caves." As the figures strode closer, Morgan recognized one of them. "They're definitely here because of the Ark."

She flattened herself back against the wall, fully aware of what Natasha El-Behery was capable of should she find them. Morgan felt an overwhelming desire to fight but there were too many men to tackle, and Khal wasn't up for the challenge. She looked around. No choice.

"We need to hide," she said.

There were a few large boulders at the back of the cave, nothing substantial, but they were better than nothing. Khal shrugged.

"Maybe they won't look very hard. There's clearly no Ark of the Covenant in here."

Morgan smiled, appreciating his humor in a difficult situation and they both ducked down behind the boulders. Morgan tensed, ready for action, as Khal awkwardly folded his body into the small space.

They heard voices at the cave entrance, shouts in Arabic and scuffling in the dust. Morgan didn't hear Natasha's voice so evidently her second-in-command must be doing the bellowing. He told the men to search the caves in pairs and a moment later, footsteps entered the cave where they were hiding.

Morgan regulated her breathing as two pairs of footsteps approached in opposite directions around the perimeter. Torchlight threw shadows against the walls. If she and Khal remained motionless, it was possible they would be missed, but if the men came too close, they would be seen. The men chatted as they casually looked around the cave, clearly not military from their lackadaisical approach. The men met in the middle of the cave in front of the boulders and then headed back towards the entrance. Morgan relaxed a little as they walked away. They were safe.

Khal shifted position unintentionally, sending some small stones skidding across the floor. The men shouted and rushed back with torches and guns held high. Khal looked devastated as he stood with arms up, stepping forward to draw attention to himself and attempting to shield Morgan's position from view. But Morgan knew that Natasha would know they were together, so she stepped out too, hands up in surrender.

The men pushed them roughly forward out of the cave and back into the blinding sunlight. They were cuffed with plastic ties and shoved down the slope to the area in front of the cave complex. Natasha smiled when she saw them, her eyes raking up and down Khal's body.

"Dr Sierra, how lovely to see you here, and once again, you have some gorgeous male company. I can only admire your choice of partners."

Natasha stepped close to Khal and gently drew her long nails down his chest. Morgan remembered how she had hypnotized Jake in this way, her physical presence assured in her sexuality. Her breasts strained against the fabric of her top, buttons undone to reveal a hint of what was beneath,

Natasha was sexy as hell and just as dangerous. Underestimating her was a death sentence. Natasha's eyes fixed on Khal's as she spoke.

"Perhaps an offering to the Gods on this holy mountain would be appropriate, perhaps it would help us find the Ark."

A shout came from one of the caves, and Natasha turned immediately, then strode towards the sound. She looked back briefly, shouting, "Bring them."

The men pushed Morgan and Khal in front of them back toward the cave Natasha had just entered. Morgan's excitement rose, despite the danger they were in. Had they found something that would lead to the Ark? She walked ahead faster and entered the cave. Towards the back, a giant altar was highlighted by torches where Natasha was bending to examine it.

"I know you're interested, Dr Sierra, so you may as well be useful." She beckoned and Morgan approached the altar.

"It would help if I wasn't cuffed."

Natasha gave her a steely gaze. Morgan shrugged. Two could play at the cold bitch game. She bent to look at the carvings on the rock altar and realized that it wasn't an altar after all.

"This is likely a sixth century tomb," Morgan said. "Look at the carving here. The kai-ro cross symbol indicates that it is early Christian, certainly not something that would have come from the time of Jeremiah or the Ark."

"But look at this," Natasha's voice had changed and Morgan noticed the awe in it, like a child finding something new and amazing for the first time. She knew Natasha's past was enmeshed with archaeology and the love of ancient civilizations, so perhaps here they could find common ground. She went round to see what was so interesting.

On the back of the altar were earlier carvings, as if the stone had been reused for the tomb but had been something else previously. The carving was worn and faded but clearly showed a procession of priests carrying temple objects, the golden menorah and the Ark of the Covenant. It was the frieze of an ancient ceremony turned into the tomb of a wealthy Christian.

"When Jerusalem was besieged and the Temple sacked in 70AD, the menorah from the Temple was taken to Rome with the captive Jews," Morgan said.

"Yes, that is shown on the Arch of Titus in Rome," Natasha replied. "The slaves in shackles, the menorah carried high, except there was no Ark found then." Natasha's eyes were wide with excitement at the chase and for a moment, Morgan saw clarity there, a shared purpose and she had a flicker of hope that this could end well for them all. Then the shutters came down in Natasha's eyes and the tendrils of darkness took back their possession. "And there is no Ark here now."

Morgan stood her ground, unflinching, as Natasha came right up to her, her eyes searching for the truth. Morgan had nothing to hide, as she still didn't know where the Ark was either. Natasha must have realized she would get nothing else from them as she stepped back. Morgan tensed, knowing how unpredictable Natasha was. Then she saw the movement coming, a shifting of the other woman's weight as Natasha lashed out in frustration, whirling her torch.

Morgan saw the signs of the oncoming attack and she stepped forward into the wide angle of Natasha's arm in order to stop the levered end smashing into her head. Morgan rushed Natasha, holding her cuffed hands out and knocking her to the ground even as the men moved to help. Khal shouted and leapt forward as they went down and was backhanded by one of the guards for his effort.

Morgan ended up behind the tomb, her face almost hitting the rock wall as she landed. She had started the fight with some element of surprise but now she was on the dusty ground, face down and cuffed while Natasha shouted at her men to leave them alone and get away. A sharp pain hit Morgan's lower back and the blows came fast as Natasha screamed her frustration. As she twisted to avoid the next kick Morgan saw something, a series of tiny carvings near the floor. In spite of the beating, she needed to get closer.

Morgan curved her body inwards towards the wall, at once protecting her injury from more damage but also blocking the carvings from the view of the others. She compartmentalized the pain as blows rained down on her back and buttocks. Natasha wasn't hitting her head yet and seemed to be venting her frustration, rather than trying to inflict serious harm. Morgan knew that she could do a lot worse, but she only needed a few more seconds.

Now Morgan could see the tiny symbols up close. They were filled with dust but were still visible, showing the Freemasons' square and compass. They were rough carvings but still definitive. Next to them were the letters PEF and a date that looked like 1868. Disappointment flooded her, for it was likely just some graffiti by a nameless pilgrim.

The realization of her failure allowed the pain back in as her body registered the blows, and Morgan heard Khal moan from the other side of the tomb. This was turning serious and she knew what Natasha did with her enemies. She needed to think quickly.

"Hey there, stop that!" A shout came suddenly from the cave entrance. Morgan rolled towards the sound as Natasha turned, wheeling round and pulling her gun on the intruders. A priest stood there, surrounded by a large tourist group, all holding cameras and smartphones. They were videoing the inside of the cave, capturing Khal being beaten. Morgan heard Natasha swear in Arabic as she covered her face with her hand and hid her gun quickly.

"Get out of here," she shouted. "This is none of your business, priest."

The man drew himself up taller, empowered by his belief

and the support of his group, as well as the power of media.

"This is holy ground, a holy mountain," the man said with an American accent. "You will not pervert it with your violence."

Morgan sensed Natasha's conflict. She wanted to shoot him but there were too many witnesses here and she could not kill them all.

"Yalla," she said brusquely to her men. "Let's go. There's nothing here anyway. Leave them."

Natasha stalked from the cave and as she approached the crowd parted to let her through. When they saw the guns, the group moved further back but they continued to point their cameras. People were empowered by the way media could record and even stop violence now. Natasha spat at the priest as she passed, but he stood his ground. The choppers started up as they boarded and the crowd continued to film as the helicopters flew off southwards.

Morgan heard them go and finally relaxed. She made it to her knees and shuffled around to Khal as the priest came back into the cave, his concerned followers right behind. They were all talking at once, excited to have witnessed such drama on an otherwise uneventful day trip.

"Are you OK? Who were those people?"

"We don't know, Father." Morgan hung her head. "We just wanted to explore the caves and then they landed, found us here and started beating us."

Khal looked dazed. One of the men in the group pushed forward with haste.

"Let me have a look at him. I have some first aid training and he might be concussed."

Morgan sat back, not wanting to demonstrate her own field training. She knew Khal would be OK, but some care from the strangers would do him good.

"Does anyone have anything to cut these cuffs off?" she asked the group.

"I have a first aid pack with scissors," one timid lady spoke up, staring at Morgan as if she was a crazy woman. Morgan could only imagine what she looked like right now, covered in dust, blood dripping down her temple. She had glanced her head on a rock when she went down but most of her injuries would be bruising from the beating. She was going to hurt like hell in the morning.

"That would be great," Morgan smiled at her sincerely.

The woman clearly had never expected to use her little first aid pack this way but she puffed up with pride as she knelt to help. Morgan imagined how this story would play out when told back in the churches of the Mid West. She still had a soft spot for religious tourists, for they had such high hopes for their travels, and this piece of drama would be just the thing to spice up their photos of the Jordanian desert.

Cuffs off, Morgan rubbed her wrists and caught Khal's eye as he sat up. He put on his best English accent for the group.

"Thank you so much. We don't know what might have happened if you hadn't shown up."

The priest looked pleased with himself. "God led us to you. He would not allow violence on this sacred mountain."

Morgan thought it was more likely that the sound of the helicopters landing had led the nosy tourists to find them, but sometimes it was better to count your blessings. She doubted that it was the last time she would see Natasha.

"We'll help you back to the parking lot," the priest announced, taking charge of his newfound charity cases.

Morgan struggled to her feet, wheezing a little and wincing as the pain in her ribs shot through her body. Taking a mental inventory, it felt like nothing was broken, just more bruises on top of the wounds she already carried. It could have been worse, and clearly Natasha had just been warming up when the beating was interrupted. Having seen evidence of what the other woman could do with a knife,

Morgan was grateful that the group had arrived when they did.

Two men helped Khal up, getting ready to go. Thanking the woman who had helped her, Morgan went to retrieve the packs. As the others walked towards the exit, she took her smartphone and bent quickly to ground level. She snapped a few pictures of the carvings at the base of the tomb and then followed the group back out into the sun.

The priest and his group were finally persuaded to continue their tour and leave Morgan and Khal alone to recover. Morgan hid her pain and Khal stood up taller as they thanked them all, assuring them that they would report the attack to the police. Finally they were left by the car on their own, and inside the Toyota, they relaxed away from prying eyes.

"Are you OK?" Morgan whispered, aware that Khal's head would be pounding from the beating he had endured and that his eyes were closed against the desert sun. Her own body was starting to feel the effects of the injuries but she was more used to this than the academic.

"Could be better." Khal managed a weak smile. "I presume you had a plan for getting us out of there."

Morgan laughed, but it was cut off as she coughed and the pain lanced through her ribs and back. When she could speak again, she croaked.

"Of course. Who do you think called the priest?"

Khal opened his eyes. "You had no phone reception."

"Details, details." She started the engine. "We need to get you somewhere to recover. Madaba is only 30 minutes away. It's a tourist-friendly town so we can lay low and blend in with the crowds."

Khal put his head back on the car seat. "Did you get any evidence of the attack?"

Morgan held up a memory card she had taken from the camera of one of the good Samaritans. "I'll get this back to ARKANE and have Martin analyze Natasha's team."

Khal nodded and closed his eyes again. Morgan concentrated on the road, thinking of the carvings in the rock. Natasha might return after the tourists had left for the day, so she couldn't rule out the symbols staying secret for long and she had to notify Martin of the developments as soon as she could, because they might be significant. She checked her phone again but the reception was still patchy. It would have to wait until Madaba.

CHAPTER 16

Madaba, Jordan. 5.16pm

GRATEFUL FOR THE GPS in the hire car, Morgan weaved in and out the crazy traffic. Madaba was known as the 'City of Mosaics' because of the vast number of Byzantine remains. Morgan had seen pictures of the most famous, a detailed mosaic map of the Holy Land and in particular, Jerusalem. The cities weren't physically far from each other, but with the current political situation, they could have been on opposite sides of the world.

They finally pulled up to the Mariam Hotel. It was cheap and cheerful with wifi, all they needed right now. Morgan reached for her backpack and pulled out a ring from a small compartment, slipping it onto the third finger of her left hand as Khal stirred.

"We're here. Come on, time to rest, and by the way, we're married for now." Khal managed to raise an eyebrow even in his debilitated state. Morgan grinned and turned away. "Don't get too excited. I don't want to leave you alone in case you're concussed."

She always carried a plain gold ring when traveling in the Middle East because it made things much easier when asked those prying questions. Her 'husband' was usually away on business, but tonight, he would be with her.

They checked in and finally made it to a room where they could recover in peace. There was only a double bed so Khal lay down on one side of it, his face set in a grimace of pain. Morgan opened up the pack and found the first aid field kit with some hardcore painkillers.

"Here, take these." She handed the pills to Khal with a glass of water and he swallowed them. He would be unconscious soon enough, and Morgan watched as his breathing slowed and became more natural, no longer inhibited by his pain. She felt her guilt subside as he relaxed into sleep, but she felt responsible for his injuries, and it could have been so much worse. However, now he was sleeping, she could check in with ARKANE.

First Morgan sent a text to Martin Klein, telling him to expect incoming media. She connected the smartphone to the hotel wifi and emailed the photos of the carvings to Martin. Then she slipped the tourist's memory card into her own camera and scrolled to the video of the attack. She captured a series of still photographs and emailed them as well. One of them clearly showed Natasha and the face of her senior bodyguard.

She didn't send the photos that showed Khal on the ground being beaten, or her own body cowering in the corner as an enraged Natasha booted her in the ribs. As Morgan thought about it, the pain began to throb again and she felt gingerly around her still healing stab wound. She could keep it away from her consciousness for some time but then it began to seep back in. Morgan had done a lot of research and training around the psychological management of pain for the Israeli military. She knew that soldiers could function even under extreme circumstances, but sometimes you just had to give into it.

She turned the phone to silent. She would call Martin later, but she needed to sleep right now. Taking two of the super painkillers, she drank a glass of water to wash them

J.F. PENN

down. She put a chair under the door handle and pulled a chest of drawers across it for extra protection but she couldn't stay awake any longer. Her body needed recovery. Morgan checked Khal's breathing again. It was regular and even, so she slipped into the other side of the bed and within seconds, she was asleep.

DAY 6

CHAPTER 17

Madaba, Jordan. 4.32am

MORGAN WOKE WITH A start as the muezzin's call rang out across the city. The clock next to the bed said it was just after 4am, so it was Fajr, the pre-dawn prayers. She and Khal had slept for more than ten hours, so clearly they had needed the rest. She reached for her phone to see five text messages and seven missed calls.

"Morning." Khal's voice was rough with sleep and the aftermath of recovery. Morgan turned to see his silhouette in the half light from the street lamps outside.

He lay on his side facing her, the sheet pulled down to his waist. Sometime in the night he must have shed his clothes for his chest was bare, and shadows highlighted the clearly defined muscles. Morgan relaxed back onto the pillow and looked at him. She was still at the opposite side of the bed and if she remained there, it would be fine. But if she touched him ... she tried to slow her breathing. The aftermath of violence and near death always felt this way. The invigorating knowledge that you were alive, that your body still functioned, that there was air in your lungs.

Khal reached out and gently traced along her arm with a fingertip. The sensation was delicious, even though her body still ached with pain. His eyes met hers. She could see the invitation there, and she knew that it was her decision to make. For a moment she thought of Jake, and then she pushed him from her mind. This was Jordan, this was now. She moved across the bed into Khal's arms.

The smartphone continued to vibrate. They had ignored it earlier but now the street was bustling outside and it was officially daytime.

"I have to get it this time," Morgan said, giving Khal's shoulder a little bite. His skin was just delicious.

"Of course, I'll shower." Khal sat up slowly, his body still protesting from the pain and the more active morning he had experienced. Morgan watched as he walked naked to the bathroom, his taut buttocks and long legs an attractive sight. Tearing her eyes away, she picked up the phone as the sound of running water started from the bathroom.

"Where have you been, Morgan? I've been calling all night." Martin's voice was concerned but also excited. He rattled off the times he had called.

"Sorry Martin, we had a bit of a run-in with Natasha and her boys. You saw the photos."

"Are you okay? And Doctor El-Souid?"

Morgan couldn't help but smile at Khal's more official title.

"We're recovered - almost - some breakfast wouldn't hurt. But what did you think of the pictures I sent?"

Martin's excitement was off the charts as he embarked on a monologue that Morgan struggled to keep up with.

"You found two interesting carvings," he said. "One clearly shows the Freemasons' symbol of square and compasses and the other, the letters PEF. We think that stands for Palestine Exploration Fund, a British Society that had tenuous links with ARKANE at the time, so we have all their records. We didn't know to look there before, but you may have found the key, Morgan. The purpose of the PEF was to investigate the archaeology, culture and natural history of the Holy Land back in the 19th century when it hadn't yet been completely explored. It wasn't a religious society but it investigated religious sites."

Morgan interrupted. "OK, but what has the PEF got to do with the Ark or the Freemasons?"

"Assume for a moment that the Ark *was* hidden there by Jeremiah," Martin said, "and clues were left in the Temple at Jerusalem. Well, between 1867 and 1870 excavations were carried out at the Temple Mount by Sir Charles Warren. He was an officer in the British Royal Engineers and also a Freemason. On his return to London, he moved up the ranks of the Freemasons and became London Metropolitan Police Commissioner during the time of the Jack the Ripper murders."

Morgan was confused.

"I still don't know what this has to do with the Ark, Martin?"

"We have the official records of the expedition to Jerusalem but I also managed to get hold of the private records that were never publicized. It seems that Warren took a side trip to Jordan and notes an item of significance found near Mount Nebo. He doesn't go into detail about the object, but he does inscribe a Bible verse on the page. 2 Samuel 6:14"

Morgan interrupted, her recall of the verse clear. "'David danced before the Lord with all his might.' It's when the Ark of the Covenant entered Jerusalem."

"Exactly," Martin's voice sounded triumphant. "But it seems that the PEF was kept in the dark about the side trip and Warren may have used what he found to advance his own career. We know for sure that he got the top job in London after his return, but the whereabouts of what he found is unknown."

"You have an idea?" Morgan asked.

"Of course, but you're going to have to come back to London to investigate it further. You need to hurry as well, because we've had reports that Natasha and her team returned to the caves after you left. She may have the same information." Morgan heard tapping on the keyboard. "I can get you on a private flight from Amman at 10.15am."

Khal came out of the bathroom with a towel wrapped around his slim waist. His hair was wet and droplets of water glistened on his muscled chest. He smiled at Morgan, his eyes bright with suggestion.

"I'm going to need a little longer than that," she whispered.

Jordanian air space. 11.38am

The private charter flight back to London gave Morgan some time to reflect on the past few days, and how quickly her relationship with Khal had developed under the pressure of the hunt for the Ark. He was making his own way back to Egypt now, and she knew that they may not see each other again, even though her body still sang with the memory of his touch. It had been too long since she had felt so alive in a man's arms.

But Morgan understood the reality of her own life now, her need for independence and her fear of loving again after what had happened to Elian. Her thoughts flickered back to the events of Pentecost and how the people she loved suffered as a result of her chosen path. How close she had gotten to Jake, and then his hideous injuries at Sedlec. She shook her head. She couldn't let Khal in any further, and he was better off without her anyway.

Pushing aside her thoughts, Morgan opened the laptop available for use by passengers and logged onto the secure ARKANE connection, accessing Martin's files about the PEF and the possible excavation of the Ark. If it had been discovered in the 19th century, it had been an amazing feat to keep it secret for so long, she thought. It was time to widen the resource net. She called up Skype and dialed Father Ben Costanza, her friend and mentor at Blackfriars in Oxford.

"Morgan, how lovely to hear from you," Ben said as he answered on the second ring, the tiny video screen filling with his old face. Morgan smiled to see him, for after her own father died, he had become the person she most trusted. He was also one of the most learned of her colleagues, and even though ARKANE had powerful databases, Ben had the benefit of many decades on earth, his mind a catalogue of things never written down.

"I'm sorry to bother you, Ben, I know it's still early there."

"Anytime, you know that. I've been worried since I found out that you discharged yourself from the hospital early. Now it looks like you're gadding about on another mission. What's going on?"

Ben was frowning with concern and Morgan could feel his eyes searching her own for the truth. He had a past with ARKANE, and she knew that he disapproved of her working for them. He had been attacked during the hunt for the Pentecost stones, but he continued to help her. Theirs was a bond not easily broken.

Morgan told him about the hunt for the Ark, and what they had found so far, omitting the X-rated details of sex and violence that had happened along the way. Ben was intrigued, as she had known he would be, for what theologian could resist the Ark of the Covenant?

"I've been watching the news from Israel, of course," Ben said. "There's been an escalation of violence in the past few days, but I had no idea that this was behind it. What do you need from me?"

"I'm emailing you the file Martin compiled which links the Ark with the British Freemasons. I wondered if you could have a look while I'm in the air, and if there's anything you can think of, let me know. We don't have much time, because the Peace Summit signing is tomorrow and that's the deadline for the appearance of the Ark in Jerusalem. Martin has been trawling the databases, but you know how secretive the Masons are."

Ben nodded, as he wrote something on the pad beside his computer.

"I might know just the person who could help us, Morgan. Come home now and I'll meet you in London this afternoon. It's only a short train ride and I could do with getting out of the College."

After the call ended, Morgan took two more heavy pain-killers and reclined her chair backwards to get a few more hours' sleep before landing. Her body was on the edge of collapse, but her drive to see Natasha stopped and violence in Jerusalem avoided would keep her going just a bit longer.

CHAPTER 18

London, England. 3.23pm

COMMUTERS HURRIED THROUGH LINCOLN'S Inn Fields, their hurried footsteps beating the pulse of London as they rushed between the offices of Holborn and Aldwych. Father Ben Costanza was past the age of swift movement so Morgan held his arm and they strolled along the street behind the park. He had insisted that they alight from the taxi on Kingsway so that they could walk a little, but she was shocked to find him so slow. The last few months had taken a toll on them both.

Ben breathed heavily as he shuffled along but his eyes were bright and alert as he looked around at the old buildings. The large public square had once been part of fashionable London in the eighteenth century, when great men lived in the townhouses. Now the barristers' chambers, the London School of Economics and the Royal College of Surgeons made the square an academic oasis in a city of hedonism and wealth.

"It's not far now," Ben pointed down the street. "Number 12 and 13, the Sir John Soane Museum."

At the pace they were walking, they had some time yet and Morgan wanted to know more about the connection Ben had uncovered.

"Tell me more about John Soane," she asked. "Who was he?"

"Born in 1753, he was the son of a humble bricklayer and yet rose to become one of England's greatest architects. He was Architect to the Bank of England and the Office of Works, so he was responsible for the government and royal buildings in Whitehall and Westminster. Soane was also a great collector and spent his wife's fortune on acquiring sculpture, paintings and objects of beauty from around the world, storing them here in a house he converted to his particular needs."

"And what is the connection to Sebastian Northbrook?"

"Sir Sebastian, my dear. He's quite particular about that."

Morgan nodded, with a smile. "Don't worry, I'll watch my manners."

"Sir Sebastian is the current Curator of the Museum, but it's a little known fact that he's also the heir to the fortune, or at least he would be if it hadn't been given to the nation in an Act of Parliament in 1833. Soane gave directions that the house must be kept as he left it so Sebastian can't touch the wealth. However, the Act was a great thing, as Soane's collection has been left intact and you'll find the place a treasure trove. I'll have to drag you back out when it's time to leave."

Ben laughed, his levity making Morgan smile. They were still under a tight deadline but this was a moment to savor their friendship and enjoy a little adventure together. Ben continued.

"There are secrets at the Soane house and Sebastian knows of many that are kept from the official records. I first came here almost 30 years ago to research some ancient texts and we spent a good many hours drinking Remy Martin Louis XIII cognac under the watchful eyes of the Lares, the gods of the house."

Morgan raised an eyebrow. "All in the name of research, I presume?"

"God loves to watch old friends enjoying the fruits of the vine together," Ben said, smiling. "We solved many mysteries of the Universe during that time. Although we haven't seen each other much recently, there are things we spoke about under the blessing of that golden liquid that suggest Sebastian knows something about the Ark so it's time to call in a few favors. Here we are."

The house was only distinguishable from the others in the row by the plaque on the gate announcing the entrance to the Museum. It was a terraced house with high, arched windows, its white facade enhanced by partial columns in the Grecian style, while statues on the third level balcony stared down with disdain at the mortals beneath. Ben raised the brass knocker on the heavy door. As he let it fall, the door opened inward.

"Benjamin, Benjamin, it's been so long, my friend. Come in, come in."

Sir Sebastian Northbrook was thin and angular, exquisitely turned out, his white hair combed back with a side parting he had probably worn since his days at Eton and Oxford. He was exactly what Morgan would have expected from a British aristocrat. "And you must be Dr Morgan Sierra." He waved them in.

"Sir Sebastian." Morgan held out her hand, but he pulled her into a brief embrace.

"No need to stand on ceremony, my dear," he said. "Benjamin tells me you're practically family, so welcome to my home, or at least it is my home until the public come back tomorrow." He sighed and Morgan caught a glimmer of the frustration born of years living with this strange arrangement. "Come and see the place."

They entered through the study, the walls a rich Pompeiian red, ringed by bookcases stacked with leather bound first editions. Morgan noticed the antique chairs that bordered the room, each with a thistle on the seat as a way to discourage tourists from resting on the precious pieces.

"Come through. I know you have some classical educa-tion Morgan, so you'll love it here."

Sebastian pulled open a pair of narrow doors at the back of the salon to reveal a tiny corridor lined with pictures, engravings and paintings. It was lit with skylights cut into the walls and ceiling. Outside the window, a rectangular courtyard with classical sculpture and a water garden was reminiscent of a Roman villa.

The corridor emerged into a gallery, packed from floor to coffered ceiling with classical statues, casts of busts, original sculptures and objects from every historical era. Morgan gaped at the scene. Here was the goddess Sekhmet, a lion-headed stone figure that looked out over the riot of antiquities. There were slave manacles, rusty and worn, as if hacked from the body of the non-person inside them. Chinese dragon dogs played alongside basalt obelisks and a black marble head of Jupiter, six times life-size, gazed out with unfathomable eyes. A huge statue of Apollo looked down into the basement below, while relief friezes of con-quest lined the walls about the god.

It was a labyrinth of early civilization, laid out in some kind of chaotic order, but her sense was of being over-whelmed. The brain was unable to process the sheer number of antiquities, the eye given no obvious place to linger in the face of so much choice. Morgan felt an urge to forget the Ark quest and immerse herself in this well of culture instead. To any lover of the classics, this was a kind of heaven.

"Is this all real?" she asked, well aware that the British of the Empire had done much salvaging of artifacts from throughout the world, some of it gathered through official means, kept safe and of benefit to future generations, but much of it ill-gotten and looted.

"Soane was a man who always got what he wanted," said Sebastian. "But sometimes all he wanted was a cast, so many of the moldings you see are casts from the original. He was a poet of architecture, enamored of the Egyptian, Greek and Roman empires in particular. The juxtaposition of the objects here was calculated to produce a particular impression. Architecture was, for him, the queen of the fine arts, with painting and sculpture as her handmaids. Together they combine, and this place showcases his vision of the mighty powers of music, poetry and allegory. But come downstairs to the basement and see the real jewel."

Sebastian slipped down some stairs, hidden behind yet more classical sculpture.

"I'll remain here, it's too steep for me" Ben said. "I can hear you from the balcony. Go on." He indicated that Morgan should follow.

She descended into semi-darkness, but as her eyes adjusted she saw that the basement was crowded with yet more precious objects. Pale natural light streamed in through the skillful use of light wells cut into the walls, both vertical and horizontal, reflected in a series of mirrors. On sunny days, Morgan could see that the light would permeate into the nooks and crannies of this basement, alighting on the faces of long dead gods frozen in stone for centuries. Today, clouds muted the light, giving a ghostly pall to the figures within. Morgan startled a little as she passed a skeleton hanging in a closet, its bones a fused androgyny of male and female in a sculpted abomination.

"Where are you, my dear?" Sebastian's voice called as Morgan rounded the corner. In front of her was a giant sarcophagus, carved from creamy alabaster. "Behold the sarcophagus of Seti I, purchased by Soane when the British Museum declined it because of lack of funding."

"Gorgeous, isn't it." Ben's voice came from above and Morgan looked up to see him gazing down into the sarcophagus from the classical balcony above. "Inside is a carving of the goddess Nut, who ruled the sky and the night.

She protected the dead as they entered the afterlife and was the barrier separating chaos from order in the world."

Morgan ran her fingers over the hieroglyphics carved on the inside of the sarcophagus. She wished for a moment that Khal was here with her, for he would know what these words meant. Sebastian pointed inside.

"It's the story of the soul's passage to the underworld. I wanted to show you the place so that you would understand what the past meant to Soane."

Morgan nodded.

"He was clearly obsessed with the classical world and ancient civilizations, so did that carry through to an interest in the Ark?"

"Soane was a Freemason," Ben's voice again came from above.

"And not just any Freemason," Sebastian continued. "He was the Grand Superintendent of Works for the Freemasons during the height of his architectural powers in London. The United Grand Lodge of England is just around the corner, and he was instrumental in remodeling the hall and kitchens, but he also designed an Ark of the Covenant to be used in ceremonies. It's nothing like the biblical Ark in design but it was constructed for a secret purpose and officially it was destroyed during the great fire of 1883." Sebastian paused. "But I know it is still kept hidden in the heart of the Lodge and I can tell you where."

CHAPTER 19

United Grand Lodge of England, London. 4.48pm

MORGAN STARED UP AT the imposing facade of the Grand Lodge of England, whose Grand Masters were always from the Royal Family. Art Deco tiers rose towards the London sky in memory of those Freemasons who had fallen in World War Two. It was an ivory mausoleum housing not a secret society, but a society with secrets. Surprisingly, the building was open to the public, with tours that ran several times daily, assuaging the need to see inside a place that had engendered so many myths.

Morgan entered and registered for the 5pm tour, walking up the wide staircase to the first floor where the library and museum were waiting to be explored. She felt strange without her gun, but the security measures meant she needed to enter clean.

She distracted herself by looking around for hints of what lay within this place. She saw door handles featuring the six pointed star of David, the seal of Solomon, and stained glass windows displaying the Latin motto, 'avdi vide tace', meaning 'Hear, See, Be Silent'. Morgan knew that conspiracy theories were rife about the Freemasons, but the top echelons of the organization were silent indeed, so was it possible that she could find one of their greatest secrets tonight?

The corridors reminded Morgan of a school, with function rooms off to the sides and great racks of coat stands for the thousands of members who would attend the Grand Temple on certain occasions. The toilets were unisex, reminding her that mainstream Masonic lodges didn't allow women, although there were women working in the Library and Museum, as well as within charities administered by the Masons.

Freemasonry was rooted in the architectural symbolism of the stonemason, and Morgan recognized many of the motifs in the regalia displayed in the museum, the square and compasses most commonly seen. Judaeo-Christian images were dominant in the articles of ceremony on show in the museum, and Morgan knew that one of the fundamental requirements of the Masons was a belief in a Supreme Being.

The Museum was carefully organized with swords and ritual objects in glass cases, as well as paintings and wax figures of the previous Grand Masters. Banners and standards hung from the balconies above.

"All those on the 5pm tour, come closer please."

The guide speaking was an older man with a Yorkshire accent. As he gathered the large group together, he spoke with pride but no arrogance, explaining how the Grand Lodge had come into being when the disparate Lodges in England had joined together. He described the architecture of the building, built with a steel frame and deep foundations so that it would continue to stand even in disaster as a fitting memorial to the soldiers who perished in war.

The guide pointed out of the window so they could look down on the triangular garden, before leading them through some preparation rooms to a high-ceilinged lobby. Morgan noted that there was just one guide for the large group of around forty people, so clearly they didn't expect any security issues.

"This is the entrance to the Grand Temple."

The guide paused and Morgan looked up to a ceiling of gold leaf and blue diametric patterns, lit by a chandelier with arms shaped like the scrolls of the Torah. Glancing down, she could see that the floor was patterned with turquoise lapis lazuli, the blue of ancient Egypt and her thoughts flickered to Khal, now so far away.

"These doors each weigh 1700 kilograms," the guide continued. "They are made of solid bronze, the panels representing the story of the building of the Temple of Solomon."

Morgan gazed over the shoulders of others in the group and had to suppress a gasp, for the top left hand panel showed the Ark of the Covenant being carried into the Temple, as a priest lay prostate before it.

The other seven panels showed aspects of the building of Solomon's Temple. Oxen and camels bore the materials needed for the structure as blocks and pillars were shifted into place by muscle-bound workers. Metal was poured into molds and women wove rich tapestries to hang over the divine sanctuary of the Holy of Holies. Priests carried the sacred menorah into the Temple, while children and worshippers sang and played instruments behind them.

Sheaves of corn flanked the door in pillars that rose to the ceiling, symbolizing new life and resurrection. Above the door the Hebrew character Yod, representing Jehovah, exuded rays of light that stretched to touch the twin globes of the celestial and terrestrial earth. It was a sensory overload of symbolism and Morgan's mind raced as she realized how much was contained in just these panels.

"Welcome to the Grand Temple," the guide said, as he swung open the heavy doors, revealing a huge open hall with a ceiling that stretched up at least sixty feet to a canopy of painted stars. The group walked in and sat in plush blue chairs facing the centre of the room. At first glance, it felt like a church or possibly a government chamber, but then

Morgan started to notice symbols hidden in plain sight.

A carpet of black and white squares approached a dais on which sat the Grand Master's throne. Around the ceiling was a mosaic frieze and above the Masonic throne was another depiction of the Ark of the Covenant. Two Ionic pillars were flanked by the figures of King Solomon and Hiram, the architect of the Temple. Between the pillars shone the golden Ark, with the wings of the Mercy seat and the carrying poles clearly defined. From the Ark, Jacob's Ladder stretched to heaven towards the Hebrew letter Yod contained in a sunburst of bright gold. On the ladder were the symbols of the Volume of Sacred Law as well as the cross for faith, the anchor for hope and the burning heart for charity. Morgan was amazed at the detail of the mosaic and tuned back in to listen to the guide's commentary.

"The Ark of the Covenant reveals God's promise to David," he said, "and it is through that promise that we receive God's continued mercy for our many sins. It is the reason that Solomon's Temple was built."

As she glanced around the room, Morgan saw more evidence of the influence of Judaism as well as of paganism and other faiths. On the frieze above, Helios the sun god rode across the sky while the All Seeing Eye of the Almighty looked down upon the crowd. The alchemical ouroboros was displayed, the snake eating its own tail in a never-ending, perfect circle of infinity and rebirth. Above her, the six pointed Star of David, the seal of Solomon, dominated the frieze.

Morgan noted that behind the throne to the left was a door behind which Sebastian had said the Ark was now kept. Hidden in plain sight indeed. She looked away, not wanting her interest to be noted. It was a fascinating place and Morgan wanted to stay and soak up the atmosphere, but the tour would soon be over, so she had to make her move. She began to cough, gently at first and then with a wracking wheeze that almost became a retch. She stood up and waved apologetically to the guide as she made her way to the door, still coughing.

"Don't worry," the guide said, waving her out, "we're almost done. Just go back to the library and they'll get you some water."

Slipping out the door, Morgan saw another couple of guides standing further down the corridor. Turning away, she continued to cough and made her way to the nearest bathroom.

Once inside, she pulled out her smartphone, navigating the plans as Martin had discovered that the modern bathrooms had been constructed with space above and behind for air to circulate and some of the ceiling tiles could be lifted. Morgan climbed up onto one of the toilets and pushed upwards on the tile. It didn't move, so she tried the next one. That didn't move either. Moving to the last stall, Morgan tried again and this time the tile shifted.

She breathed a sigh of relief for there were only a few minutes before the tour would be over. Martin would hack into the system and make sure her pass was tagged so it looked like she had left with the other visitors at the end of the day, but she couldn't be caught in here.

She threw her small backpack into the space above and pulled herself up. She had just carefully replaced the tile over the hole as the bathroom door opened and she could hear the voices of other people. The door banged again soon after and she breathed more easily, for now all she had to do was wait.

DAY 7

CHAPTER 20

Grand Lodge of England, 2.34am

MORGAN HAD LEARNED THE skill of silent waiting without sleeping in the military. Nevertheless, lying in the dark regulating her breathing for hours had brought her to the brink of exhaustion. Sebastian had told her that the night shift consisted of low-level security guards, but Morgan had still wanted to wait until after 2am when the guards in the atrium would be sleepy and relaxed.

Stretching her muscles, Morgan eased the tile away and dropped down into the bathroom stall, pulling it back over to cover where she had been hiding. She switched on her pen torch, then pulled out a tiny microphone and put it in her ear. She tapped it twice.

"Morning, Morgan." Martin's voice yawned in her ear.

She tapped it twice again for she would only speak if really necessary. Martin was tracking her on the GPS through the building and he also had heat sensors of the guards, so he could warn her of anyone approaching. He had hacked into the security systems, looping them so that she could move undetected through the building.

They had decided to keep the incursion a secret from Director Marietti, mainly because they weren't sure the Ark was really here, and given the time pressures, it was easier to seek forgiveness later than to ask for permission. Morgan had told Martin that the visit was for reconnaissance, and if she found the Ark, he would call Marietti to alert the official channels.

Morgan pulled open the bathroom door and listened. Nothing. She knew that the great bronze door to the Temple was held on special hinges so that it swung easily despite its massive weight, but first she had to locate the key. Sebastian had been a keeper of the key at one point in his Masonic career and he had told her that it was kept in the Museum. It was an antique, precious in its own right.

Morgan slipped into the atrium outside the Grand Temple, her tiny light picking out the gold leaf in the interlocking stars on the mosaic floor, and then the glint of bronze reflected from the gigantic door. She swiftly padded back through the corridors towards the Museum.

Entering quietly through the double doors, Morgan was struck by how crowded the space was. She shone her light around the gallery where the seats of the past Grand Masters sat regally, and paintings of men long dead stared back at her.

"It's in a case under the standard with the parrots." Martin's voice seemed loud in the silence but Morgan knew it was only in her ear. "It's officially Argent a Fesse Gules between three Parrots Vert, if you want the heraldry explanation. Belongs to the Earl of Scarborough, Grand Master in the 1950s, whose son …"

Morgan tapped her ear again, and Martin went quiet. "Sorry," he whispered. "I'm excited to be out in the field with you."

Morgan smiled and shone her torch at the banners hanging from the balcony, richly embroidered with the coats of arms of previous Grand Masters. Her torch illuminated three bright green parrots, strangely out of place against the dark wood that dominated the room. Underneath was a glass case.

"The case is locked from the top but should have a side panel that slides open," Martin said softly.

Morgan shone her torch into the case, lighting a long, ornate key decorated in Art Deco style with lilies on flowing water. She felt along the side of the case and it slid open, the mechanism so smooth it was clearly used every day. She reached in and took the key. It was heavy and cold, awkward in her hand. Closing the case, she tapped her mic gently and headed back towards the Grand Temple. So far, so good, Morgan thought, daring to hope that the next steps would go as smoothly.

She walked back to the Temple through corridors pooled with moonlight colored by the stained glass windows. Morgan turned off her torch and paused a moment, listening to the silence. She felt a touch of the sacred there, a sense of faith and belief that permeated the building. One of the windows showed a woman portrayed in glass mosaic, the embodiment of charity. Despite the fact that mainstream Lodges didn't accept women, they certainly had a place here.

"Are you okay?" Martin's voice came in her ear, interrupting her thoughts. Morgan tapped her mic gently and moved towards the great doors of the Temple, suddenly feeling as if she was trespassing, an outsider breaching a sacred place. Forgive us our sins, she thought and fitted the key into a keyhole totally out of scale with the gigantic bronze doors. She looked up at the top left panel, the Ark of the Covenant resplendent as it entered Solomon's Temple surrounded by priests. How much of this was allegory, she wondered, and how much was truth altered by time? Morgan turned the key and pushed.

The door swung open silently, a portal to the inner Temple. She stepped inside, edging the door shut behind her, feeling tiny in the giant space. Her torchlight didn't reach the ceiling, but moonlight flooded through one side of the hall through tall stained glass depicting rays streaming from heaven to the blue earth. Morgan took a deep breath and approached the throne of the Grand Master, resplendent in the centre of a dais at the front of the room. It was an ornate gold monstrosity, the type of archetypal throne a child would draw for a King in a fairy story. Above it was a canopy of gold, and on either side two lower chairs of yellow and blue brocade.

She moved to the throne as Sebastian had said there was a key to the inner sanctum in the Master's chest which sat in front of the throne. It was shaped like an altar, with the Egyptian uraeus, stylized cobra heads, on each side. Morgan gripped the heads and lifted.

The chest swung open to reveal the tools of the Grand Master lying inside, embedded in a blue velvet tray designed to fit snugly within. Each tool was highly decorated and embossed with gold filigree. The square and compasses, which Morgan knew to represent virtue and wisdom of conduct, the trowel for spreading the cement of kindness between brothers, and the gavel as emblem of authority. Morgan picked up the gavel and hefted its weight. It was surprisingly heavy for something symbolic. She gazed down at the other tools, wondering what they were used for, but nothing seemed sinister despite the reputation of the Masons.

"Have you found the key?" Martin's voice was insistent in her ear.

Morgan replaced the gavel and lifted the tray out of the chest completely, revealing another layer beneath with tools of ancient wood laid on a piece of chestnut colored leather. In the middle was a key, in itself quite normal looking, but the way it was placed, surrounded by sacred objects, demonstrated its importance.

She picked the key up and tapped her mic once, before

turning towards the door on the right of the throne. The door looked as if it led to an ante-room for disrobing or something similar, but over the door was the Hebrew Yod character representing God, and Morgan felt a sense of trepidation as she turned the key in the lock.

On the other side, a short corridor opened out into a circular chamber, and in the centre was John Soane's tribute Ark, said to have been destroyed in the fires of 1863, but clearly saved and kept secret ever since. Morgan knew that officially it had been the repository for the Articles of Union, when the two great Lodges came together under one banner, but that had evidently been just one part of the story.

The room was hung floor to ceiling with rich tapestries, vividly depicting the building of the Temple of Solomon, giving the room a muted feeling of being cocooned in rich fabric. Soane's Ark was about four feet high, a triangular classical structure with miniature Doric, Ionic and Corinthian columns representing wisdom, strength and beauty. It was plain with no decoration, like an austere tomb, with three steps topped with kneeling cushions leading to a pair of double doors. Thick candles burned either side and the scent of incense hung in the air.

Whatever this was, Morgan thought, it definitely did not hold the Articles of Union, for surely they wouldn't be worshipped in this way.

"Is it there?" Martin's voice in her ear betrayed his excitement.

Morgan knelt on the top step and pulled open the double doors. They swung outwards to reveal a gold chest with two cherubim on top, their wings meeting in the middle where the presence of God would sit. Morgan's heart was thumping now, but this chest couldn't be the real Ark because it was too small and looked relatively new. She pulled a small webcam from her bag and mounted it on her torch, so Martin could see what she was looking at.

"Oh wow, is that it?" he said.

Morgan signaled 'unsure' with her hand in front of the camera. Bracing the torch, she felt a moment of unease, a hesitation at revealing what could be the most important relic of Judaism. Whatever her personal doubts about religion, the Ark was of crucial historical importance. Taking a deep breath, she leaned forward and opened the chest.

Inside lay four objects. A length of hardwood with gold inlaid on one surface, a palm sized fragment of stone with chiseled words on it, a vial filled with white flakes and a piece of rounded staff.

"The Ark contained the tablets of the Law, manna from heaven and Aaron's Rod," Morgan whispered aloud as the sound of rushing waters filled the room, like a celestial waterfall. She suddenly felt an overwhelming wave of emotion as her thoughts raced through stories of her childhood, snapshots of an old faith. She wanted to weep and prostrate herself here, not caring about being found, only desiring to be in the presence of these sacred things. She reached out her hand to touch the piece of the true Ark.

"Morgan, there's trouble out here."

Martin's voice broke her concentration and she jerked her hand back, shaking her head to dispel the emotions that threatened to overwhelm her. What just happened? Morgan wondered. The rational part of her mind tried to examine what was going on, even though she could still feel the tremors of emotion within her.

"A van just pulled up to the entrance." Martin's voice was frantic now. "Oh hell, Morgan they've just rammed the doors." A sound of muffled gunfire came from below. "It looks like there are six of them. They have guns. Morgan, you've got to get out of there."

She spoke into the mic.

"The Ark is here Martin, or at least fragments of it. I can't leave this here for them to take."

Martin was almost shouting now. "I can see from the cameras they're on their way up to you. Get out, Morgan, please. Just leave, we can't deal with this ourselves."

The gunfire had stopped, but Morgan could hear muffled sounds of crashing and banging coming closer. This was no stealth mission, just a determined, violent attempt to snatch the Ark. She looked around for some kind of weapon but only the large candlesticks looked to be of any use. She tried to lift one but it was too heavy.

Morgan turned to the tapestries, pulling one back to reveal a slim alcove behind it. She squatted down low and calmed her breathing again, hearing voices in the Temple as the bronze door was pushed open. A guard was begging for his life even as he led the intruders towards the sanctuary. The voices drew closer and then they were in the room.

"The Ark has already been opened, so much for your secrets." There was a crack of metal against bone, a grunt and the noise of a body dropping to the floor. Morgan recognized that voice. Natasha El-Behery had found her again.

"Dr Sierra, I know you're in here. Your so-called genius tech guy is no match for my hacker resources, and we've been shadowing your Freemason research with interest." The voice came smooth as honey, then gunshots peppered the room, shredding the tapestries in a wide arc at shoulder height. Morgan crouched as low as she could while bullets ripped into the wall above her head. She shuffled down even further until she was almost lying at the bottom of the alcove as Natasha continued. "When I found a piece of the Ark in Ethiopia, I knew that it would be difficult to trace the other pieces, but you found the key for us in Jordan. The Freemasons have the rest of them, split between the Lodges in England as a symbol of their power."

The bullets came again, this time at waist height, barely missing Morgan as they pockmarked the wall behind her. She pulled the mic from her ear, placing it just under the corner of the tapestry facing into the room. She knew Martin would be trying to call for backup but at least there would be evidence of what was happening to her.

"The other fragments are being collected as we speak. My men are raiding lodges up and down the country, and soon the Ark will be fitted together again. It will return in triumph to Jerusalem, which will drown in blood because of it, but you'll have to miss that happy event."

Morgan's heart was thumping with anger and frustration as well as fear but she didn't want to cower behind this cloth, waiting to die within the shroud of the Temple. She rolled out from under the tapestry. Two men grabbed her and held her fast while two others stood in the shrine along with Natasha. She was dressed in black leather, her long hair tied into a slick bun, bright red lipstick on her mouth. A painted doll, and a brutal killer.

"There you are," Natasha purred as she took a step back. "Hold her."

She signaled to one of the men next to her. He grinned, a leer of anticipation on his face as he put down his gun and stepped towards Morgan. She braced herself for what was to come, not wanting to give Natasha the satisfaction of watching her flinch.

The man's fist exploded into the side of her face. Another punch came quickly and she grunted as blood gushed from her nose and her mouth filled with the salty tang. She coughed and spat but barely managed to take a breath before he punched her in the solar plexus, the intense pain amplified by the knife wound that had not healed completely.

Morgan doubled over, winded and sagging in the arms of the men who held her. Natasha stepped close and bent down, trailing a finger across Morgan's lips, covering them with her own blood.

"Taste this and know you will die here." She straightened again. "But a bullet is too good for you and we don't have time to beat you to death, although I would have enjoyed watching it. So you will burn, tied to Soane's Ark as a testament to your failure."

Morgan squashed the pain into a corner of her mind, trying to focus on what was happening. She could see through a haze of tears and blood that two of the men were carrying the smaller gold chest containing the pieces out into the main Temple. She felt a great tug of emotion at seeing it leave. There was certainly something supernatural in there, for the emotions it stirred resonated deep within her.

"You can't win, Natasha," Morgan managed to speak although her jaw was throbbing with pain. "The Ark is too strong, even for you. I know you can feel its pull."

Natasha turned in surprise. "Even you believe in this magic? I'm surprised, for I thought you were a woman of science. But this is just another piece in a religious conspiracy and I'm taking it to where it belongs."

"The Ark can't go back to Israel," Morgan pleaded. "The country will rip itself to pieces fighting over it."

Natasha smiled. "There are many who would celebrate that consequence. Enough now. Tie her."

One of the men stuffed a piece of shredded tapestry into Morgan's mouth, as they pushed her against Soane's Ark and wound more of the material around her, binding her to it. Natasha's eyes took on a wicked gleam.

"Wait," she said. "Hold out her hand."

Morgan struggled in their grasp but the men held her steady. They stretched her left arm out, pinning her wrist. Natasha pulled out an ornate sacrificial knife.

"This was in the Museum, just down the hall. I thought it would go nicely in my own collection but perhaps it should stay here with you."

She caressed Morgan's clenched fist with her fingertips, and then slashed at her knuckles with the knife. The pain was delayed for a millisecond but then Morgan gasped as the agony flashed through her.

"Open it," Natasha demanded. One of the men prised Morgan's fingers open and Natasha thrust the knife through her palm, pinning her to Soane's Ark. Morgan screamed into the gag, a roar of frustration and anger mingling with the pain. She struggled to breathe. "Your blood will drip into the empty place where the pieces of the true Ark once sat," Natasha said. "A fitting end, I think, for the inner sanctum to be desecrated by the blood and death of a woman. "

The two guards finished tying Morgan, binding her tightly. She felt the contours of Soane's Ark on her back and in the depths of her pain, she saw the guards splashing some kind of accelerant as the stink of it filled the room. They threw it over Morgan, soaking her hair, and as it dripped into her wounds, she howled through the gag as it burned on her skin.

Natasha flicked open a lighter and lit the tapestry next to the door, then she bent and lit two other places. She watched as they caught and smoke began to fill the room, smiling with a look that was almost jealousy.

"See you in Hell, Morgan. I hope you're still burning when I get there."

She stalked after the men carrying the smaller Ark.

Morgan watched her leave as the flames began to take hold and lick their way towards her, the heat already intense as the accelerant caught. She heard gunfire again, hoping that it wasn't for Martin. The smoke made her cough into the gag and the stench made her want to retch but she tried to suppress the urge. She struggled in the bonds, the pain from her stabbed hand lancing up her arm, even as she failed to loosen the ties. The Soane Ark was old, dry wood. It would burn fast and with it, she would die.

Flames reached the bottom step and Morgan shuffled her feet away as far as she could while smoke billowed from the tapestries in an acrid cloud. The first lick of flame on her skin was almost cold as it took its time to register, then suddenly it seemed that the air was filled with color. For a moment, Morgan could see heaven as Isaiah had described, the glory of God and the angels with six wings. Then the shock of pain ripped through her and her vision faded to black.

CHAPTER 21

Grand Lodge of England, 3.01am

MARTIN LISTENED TO THE disaster unfolding from the safety of the van, frozen and unsure what to do. He heard Morgan's torture and watched as Natasha and her men strode out of the broken door of the Grand Lodge, put the chest into the van and drove off into the night.

Martin knew he should do something but he didn't know what. They were on an illegal mission that the Director wasn't aware of and he didn't know the protocol for this situation. Yet, Morgan was hurt, or worse and he was just sitting here, but he couldn't do anything. He felt frozen with fear and the academic side of his brain told him that it was the freeze reflex, a survival mechanism.

Martin rocked back and forwards on his seat, thoughts tripping over themselves in his head. He was just a researcher, he shouldn't be out here, shouldn't be helping with this. It was only because he knew that this was what Jake would have done that he had agreed to it at all, but he wasn't a field agent and there was nothing he could do. But now Morgan was burning alive in the temple.

A window exploded above him, raining broken glass onto the pavement below in shards of blue heaven. Smoke billowed out and there was a whooshing sound as air swept into the building, feeding the flames.

"Morgan," Martin whispered, afraid he was leaving her to die with his indecision.

A banging shook the van door.

"Open up, Morgan's in trouble. It's Ben, we're here to help." The old man's voice was urgent as he continued to bang on the door.

Martin was finally startled from his frozen position and unlocked the door to see the priest, Father Ben Costanza, and with him, another old man.

"Where's Morgan?" Ben asked.

Martin's face blanched and he pointed to the Lodge, where bodies lay half out the door, a bloody trail of carnage left behind by Natasha and her men. Ben pulled up his cassock and started to run as fast as his old legs would carry him towards the Temple. He turned back to Martin.

"Come on, we may need your young strength."

Martin felt a flush of shame at his indecision when these two old men had no hesitation in running into the burning building. He jumped from the van, clicked the locking mechanism into place and ran after them, catching up in the lobby, as they looked around at the bodies of the guards.

"Are they alive, Sebastian?" Ben asked, hand on his chest as he wheezed.

Martin watched as the other man quickly touched his fingers to the pulse points in their necks.

"Doesn't seem like it," Sebastian said, "but I've called for the emergency services, so they should be here soon enough. Morgan must be upstairs in the temple. Come, we must hurry."

Martin ran ahead with Sebastian's trim form leading the way down the corridors. Ben slowed behind them to a walk, holding his chest and waving them ahead.

"Go, I'll catch you up. Find her, please."

Martin noticed that the place was resplendent with

symbols, mosaics and gold leaf, but all he wanted right now was to find Morgan. When he had heard them torturing her, he couldn't imagine how she could survive. Sebastian pushed the bronze doors open and they were met with clouds of billowing smoke.

"Get close to the floor and follow me," he said, dropping to his knees and crawling into the smoke filled room.

Martin stood there, looking into the dark, rolling clouds of smoke curling up to a mosaic frieze where he could see the sunburst of Jehovah about to be subsumed in flame. This was a hell made reality by evil. This was what he fought against in the cleanliness of his lab, from the distance of his laptop, with the impersonality of programming, but now it was here in the heart of London and he could avoid this confrontation no longer.

Martin fell to his knees and crawled after Sebastian, coughing as he went. It took an age to cross the marble floor and then he felt Sebastian grab his arm in the smoke, shouting over the roar of the flames.

"The Ark sanctuary is this way. I'm going in but you stay here, hold this rope. When you feel me pull it twice, haul it back out."

Martin nodded, grateful for Sebastian being there to take charge. He clutched the ceremonial rope and bent closer to the floor, where the air wasn't so thick with smoke but he could still feel the heat of the flames from the room ahead. How could anyone survive in there? Seconds passed and he wondered whether they would now lose two people instead of one. Then two sharp tugs came, almost pulling the rope from his hands.

Martin pulled hand over hand, bracing himself against the steps of what he thought must be the dais of the Temple throne. It was hard going, a dead weight. The morbid thought raced through his brain and he stamped it down. Not dead, surely, just wounded.

He moved to a crouch and started to pull back the way he had come, towards the direction of the double bronze doors. Halfway back, the weight increased again, but Martin pulled onwards, finally reaching the door. There Ben waited and together they pulled the rope out the door, revealing Morgan's bloody, black body, her hand wounded and streaked with blood. She was wrapped in a shroud of tapestry, the rope tied around her middle.

"Oh Lord," Ben cried, bending to her, feeling for her pulse. "Weak, but she's alive. Where's Sebastian?"

Martin looked back into the smoke, tendrils of soot forming the faces of demons that mocked him to return to their embrace.

"He's in there. I felt him drop. I'm going back in."

Martin crawled back into the temple, feeling his way with outstretched arms in wide arcs, trying to locate Sebastian's body in the smoke. He must have succumbed to smoke inhalation with the strain of rescuing Morgan and now Martin was the old man's only chance.

Finally, his fingertips touched cloth, then an arm. Martin grabbed the back of Sebastian's tweed jacket and pulled, dragging the man along the black and white checkered floor, inching towards the doors and safety. He wheezed and coughed and the devils of smoke wrapped their tendrils around his neck and shoved them down his throat. He retched, spitting up bile and dark clots of ash, but he pulled onwards.

Just as he thought he couldn't go on anymore, a pair of strong hands dragged him forwards and he felt another set pull Sebastian free. Martin felt an oxygen mask being placed onto his face and his body being rolled onto a stretcher. The fire service and ambulance had arrived.

Martin glanced sideways and saw Sebastian wearing a mask, and then Morgan, her face blackened with smoke. Ben was by her side, squeezing her hand, stroking her brow.

Martin could see how much he loved her and thankfully they hadn't left her to die, but they had lost the Ark.

CHAPTER 22

Jerusalem, Israel. 12 noon.

THE MALEVOLENT FORCES OF chaos gathered above the Old City as hatred and rage boiled over in the midday summer heat. The crowd started to jostle one other as they walked briskly down El Wad HaGai street towards the Western Wall, the shouting sporadic, not yet a chant.

Avi Kabede, al-Hirbaa, pulled the hood of his jacket up to shield his face as he didn't want to appear in any media reports of this event. He stayed at the edge of the crowd, instant messaging with key extremists in his team who were among the throng of right-wing extremist Jews. Technology meant that he could direct the mayhem without being part of it. He knew that they wouldn't notice a Falasha anyway, and none of the men had seen his face, they had only received his money and directions virtually.

Avi looked around the streets as he walked, noting the different faces and clothing that denoted the races that co-existed here. For in Jerusalem cultures clash, religious ideologies collide and families become collateral damage in an unending struggle. The Holy City is a cesspit of lies, violence and revenge, he thought, for the wars that rage in the human heart spill over into these streets.

The worship of God is torn into three here, Jews, Muslims

and Christians all jostling for position as their prayers mingle with one breath and curses taint the air with the next. Prostitutes of faith hawked their wares to gullible pilgrims who trekked after guides through the winding streets. It is a city that exists both on earth and as the heavenly Jerusalem, a myth perpetuated by those who return from it trying to patch lies over the truth they saw here. Avi looked around him at the crowd, a foretaste of violence in his mouth, for this was also where the great religions of the world would end in a blaze of fire when the glory of God came again.

Avi frowned as he checked his smartphone for the fifth time in as many minutes. He had been trying, and failing, to reach Natasha El-Behery for the last eight hours. In the previous communication she had confirmed that the pieces of the Ark had been recovered from the Freemason lodges of England and that the team were on a plane bound for Israel, but the plane had never arrived. Natasha and her team had vanished and with them, the Ark that he needed to galvanize the crowds into storming the Temple Mount and triggering the escalation into religious war.

But now events had been set in motion and it was too late to pull people back. After stoking the violence for days through right-wing media reports and his own special brand of extremist rhetoric, the summit signing was in two hours. Avi needed to engineer the violence to steal press attention from peace and towards the prospect of war, and he had a slim window of opportunity. He clung to the hope that Natasha would still come through as the swelling crowd marched onwards to the Wall.

Avi watched the men around him, their faces etched with anger, fists clenched and he knew that he had chosen his partners well. The Temple Mount Alliance were dedicated to building a Third Temple on the site of the first two. To do this they were intent on liberating the Temple Mount from Muslim control and destroying the existing mosque, for no

Jewish Temple could be consecrated to God there without the removal of what they considered to be offensive shrines. In the past year, Jews had been kept from the holy place, and today they were determined to take it back. Placards punctuated the air above the crowd, as shouts began to coalesce into chanting.

"Jerusalem, undivided."

"Liberate the Temple Mount."

"Shoah for the Arabs."

Avi had also used his contacts to stir unrest within the fundamentalist Muslim groups in the city, and they were waiting on the other side of the wall. Some were at prayers at the mosque and others outside the gates in the Muslim Quarter, waiting for signs of violence before they streamed in. Avi cursed Natasha, for everything but the Ark was in place, and the city teetered on a knife-edge of violence that should be sparked by this single event. If she didn't deliver the Ark as a rallying sign, the Jews on the edge of the plaza wouldn't join the violence, for most of the city sat on the fence. They preferred to keep the peace than to take by force what they quietly considered to be rightfully theirs.

It was ironic that both sets of extremists agreed on one thing - the peace talks must fail, as they had always failed before. Even after Yitzhak Rabin and Yasser Arafat had shaken hands on the White House lawn in 1993, it didn't take long before the hawks ruled Israel again. There were moments of tentative calm where it seemed as if there could be some kind of religious unity. Then a bomb blast would shatter the quiet and bodies would be pulled forth from the rubble, martyrs to the next round of the blood feud. The Second Intifada was sparked when Ariel Sharon walked onto the al-Aqsa mosque complex, and children continued to grow up with racial stereotypes and no idea of who the people on the other side of the wall really were.

Avi wondered whether the final allegiance must be

to the city itself, which stood above and beyond faith, for there could be no absolute truth when the layers of history and culture mingled so deeply. The city was built on death, cutting into its own body and self-harming until the blood of generations seeped into the earth. Perhaps today a blood sacrifice would appease the gods of the high places who once ruled here.

Avi glanced at his smartphone again, checking the time. He couldn't wait for Natasha any longer, for they were drawing near to the plaza. The crowd couldn't be restrained and they had to enter with brute force. They had kept things civil, but now it was time to rain havoc on the square in front of the Kotel, the Western Wall. He sent a flurry of messages to key individuals within the crowd.

At moments like this, he was torn by his desire to be at the head of the march, beating time on the drums as the chanting grew louder. But a greater authority lay in his anonymity, for the Temple Alliance and the extremist Muslim groups all believed that he fitted easily on their side. Avi looked up to the sky, brilliant blue studded by white clouds reminiscent of the Israeli flag. He felt that God was blessing this mission, setting his seal on a moment that would go down in history, the beginning of the end for Israel.

A yell came from the front of the march, then the rapid stamping of feet echoed through the streets as men started to run towards the Western Wall. Avi shouted along with the crowd and picked up the pace as they ducked around market stalls, spilling onto the pavements of the old city. One man tipped over a stall, igniting a trail of violence as the mob pushed over tables and kicked at vendors, breaking their wares with abandon. Some people shouted after them while others shrank back into doorways to avoid the conflict, for a mob on the run was wild and uncontrollable.

Avi glanced at his watch again. There was still time for Natasha to smuggle in the Ark while the soldiers were dealing with the riot to come. If the Ark was revealed, then at 1pm the shofar would sound across the plaza as a symbolic new beginning. The blast of the ram's horn had been heard emanating from the thick cloud of Sinai in the book of Exodus and had sounded again when the Jewish soldiers liberated the Western Wall from the Jordanians in the 1967 war. Many believed that the hard-won sacrifice had been belittled by the domination of Islam on the Temple Mount and Avi believed that it was the sound that would galvanize those on the fence. They had fifteen minutes to get into position, then, God willing, they would storm the Temple Mount.

The narrow streets of the Old City funneled protestors into a tighter mob as they approached the plaza, and Avi's phone vibrated with a message from the Muslim side. There was a group ready to defend the Temple Mount from the protestors and more waiting inside the al-Aqsa compound with weapons in place. Avi smiled, knowing that both sides were willing to die in the defense of this holy place.

The mob ran into the plaza, ugly chanting resounding in the holy place. Avi could see Israeli soldiers massing in defense at the bottom of the wooden walkway leading up to Mughrabi Gate, the only entrance to the Temple Mount compound from the Israeli side. He saw press vehicles and the reporters he had tipped off pushing their way through the curious onlookers. Avi smiled, for surely the Israeli soldiers couldn't fire on their own people, not live on TV. He knew that many of them agreed with the stance of the protestors anyway and might let them in. For there was no freedom of religious expression in this part of Jerusalem, only segregation.

The mob surged against the soldiers, who linked arms and pushed them back. As the violence took hold, batons crashed down on the protestors but their sheer numbers began pushing the Israeli forces back. The sound of shouting and grunts of effort filled the air, smothering the sound of people praying at the Wall, most of whom scuttled away from the violence.

Avi watched as a breakaway protestor made it halfway up the ramp, clearly heading for Mughrabi Gate. A shot rang out from above and he sank to the ground, clutching his chest, blood blossoming through his clothes. The shot had come from atop the walls protecting the Temple Mount. The crowd roared and surged, pushing the Israeli soldiers, who turned in horror to see the man fall. They had been ordered to stop their own people, but now the shooting of an unarmed protestor by the other side could be seen as an act of war. That moment of indecision turned the tide as the soldiers relaxed the lines and the mob surged through.

Avi fought his way to a better vantage point. The shofar should have sounded by now, but he couldn't see Natasha, or anything resembling the Ark. He cursed her incompetence and whispered revenge, but even without the Ark, this would strike a blow at the heart of the Peace Process, for the press he had called were getting plenty of footage of the exploding violence. More shots came from the walls and this time, the Israeli soldiers began shooting back. Avi knew that it wouldn't be long before reinforcements were brought in on both sides to quell the riot. They needed to get into that compound if they were to escalate the battle.

The mob had become a violent spiral of rage and they stormed the ramp together, some falling as they were picked off from above. Screams joined the shouting but the crowd didn't stop. One of the extremists grabbed a battering ram from a security outpost that had been barely defended and a few of the biggest men used it to hammer the door leading into the mosque compound. The door wasn't strong enough to resist the weight of the protestors and soon the ram smashed it open and the mob surged into the Noble Sanctuary, the Haram el-Sharif.

The chants of the crowd grew louder. One group of men ran for the Dome of the Rock, and another toward the al-Aqsa mosque, forbidden to non-Muslims. The guards of the compound began shooting, trying to stop what looked like an invasion, as extremist Muslim groups stormed into the compound bringing more weapons and calling for jihad in the name of Allah.

Avi noticed a cameraman dodge bullets and shelter behind a fountain. Bullets pinged off the enamel tiles, but he still held the camera up to capture the firefight. Avi reveled in the thought of the news footage streaming live to the world. Some of the Israeli soldiers had joined the protestors now, as Avi had foreseen they would. Inevitably the battle was splitting down racial and religious lines.

He ran with the crowd towards the Dome of the Rock, where faithful Muslims were abandoning their prayers, even as the guards defended their retreat. Avi saw the Imam come out and stand in front of the entrance, his old face crumpled with anguish at the devastation, his words of peace unheeded. He was drowned out by the roaring of the mob, a rage that could not be contained.

Avi watched in despair as the Imam was overwhelmed and kicked to the ground, disappearing under the throng who surged into the Dome. Avi cursed Natasha. This should have been the moment of triumph. If the Ark had been returned to the Temple location today, there was no way the Israelis would ever let this place remain in Muslim hands. War would have been a certainty. But without the Ark, he feared the violence today would just be portrayed as another riot of minority extremists.

When the Imam went down, Avi knew the tide would turn against them. The act would spark violence and reprisals throughout the city, but ultimately it would fail, because there was no Ark of the Covenant to unite the sides against each other for a longer-term war. Natasha El-Behery would pay for her failure, but al-Hirbaa would eventually find another way to bring down Israel.

A Muslim worshipper ran across the plaza, looking behind for fear of more violence. Avi jumped out in front of the man, swinging him into the bushes and slamming the butt of his gun into the man's temple. Quickly, he stripped off the man's outer clothing and pulled them on over his own, discarding his Jewish kippah and replacing it with a taqiyah, a Muslim prayer cap.

Emerging from the dense bush, Avi walked quickly to one of the side gates into the Muslim quarter, as young men surged from the streets below into the compound, ready to join the fight. Avi stepped aside to let them pass, for he knew there would always be another chance. Jerusalem was a city permanently on the edge of its own destruction and Avi knew that the end would come, just not today.

Al-Jazeera Broadcast, Jerusalem, Israel

The Old City of Jerusalem exploded with violence this morning with running battles between Jews and Muslims. Twelve people are reported to have been killed, seven Jews and five Muslims. The Imam of the Al-Aqsa mosque remains in critical condition tonight from injuries sustained as he tried to reason for peace. The Dome of the Rock was looted and defaced with offensive graffiti.

Israeli officials have condemned the violence as committed by marginal extremists attempting to disrupt the peace process. Some Muslim leaders are proclaiming the violence an act of religious war, and calling for the expulsion of the Jews from Jerusalem.

Calm was restored after several hours by the Israeli police

and military in what are now being called "heavy handed tactics". Tear gas was fired and the compound cleared of non-Muslims in accordance with the current law forbidding them access into the area.

At the time of the violence, the President of the United States was signing the new Peace Accords between Israel and the Palestinians in the hope of knitting together a new generation of moderates on both sides.

At the press conference, the President announced "There will always be those who seek to pervert and destroy the peace process, but we stand together today and pronounce that extremism cannot win while the majority continue to seek a peaceful solution. We have signed these accords with the support of the international community. We may not share a common religion, but we have a shared humanity and a hope for our collective future. This land belongs to Jews, Muslims and Christians, who must ultimately learn to shake hands and start anew."

Hundreds of bunches of flowers have been laid on both sides of the Western Wall today expressing messages of peace and hope.

DAY 8

CHAPTER 23

St Barts Hospital, London, England. 6.18am

THE LIGHT WAS DAZZLING, even through her closed eyelids so Morgan kept them closed, squeezing them tight against the day. Her head was pounding and she could feel a throbbing in her hand where the knife had pierced. Her chest was tight and constricted and the older wound in her side was a deep ache. Over it all, she could feel the soporific haze of painkilling drugs, but underneath her body still thrummed with hurt.

Still with her eyes closed, she reached her right hand over to her left and felt the bandages. Pressing a little, Morgan winced with the pain even as she wiggled her fingertips. They moved, so at least the attack hadn't done any major damage.

"How are you feeling?" a voice asked.

Morgan opened her eyes a fraction and saw ARKANE Director Marietti standing by the door. She tried to speak but her throat was hoarse and all that came out was a rasp.

"It's OK," he said. "Don't try to speak. You've got some recovery to do yet again, although you've been unconscious for 24 hours. Smoke inhalation can cause severe issues and you're lucky you're not burned to death. You can thank Sebastian Northbrook for that. He's in Intensive Care, by the way."

Morgan shut her eyes to shield herself from his angry glare. She hadn't known how she had escaped a fiery death in the Temple but the thought of the curator dragging her through the smoke made her weak with guilt.

"Seriously, Morgan," Marietti continued. "Didn't you think I needed to know about your mission? I could have prevented what happened. As it was, you were rescued by two pensioners and a geek, instead of a specialized ARKANE team who could have captured Natasha and secured the Ark at the same time."

Morgan could hear the anger in his voice, and she was mad at herself thinking of what Sebastian had risked for her. She hardly knew the man, but he had come to her aid and now he was critically injured. Ben must have been there too, and Martin. Her crazy backup team. Marietti was right, what had she been thinking?

She heard the chair squeak as Marietti sat in the chair by the bed, his voice was softer now.

"You're part of ARKANE now, Morgan, not some vigilante who can go after the bad guys alone. You have a team." She felt the weight of his hand gently on her arm and just for a second, she knew that he really meant the words. "It's also my fault," he continued. "I should have checked in with you but the Middle East political situation has been taking all of my attention. Now I have to deal with the wrath of British Freemasonry, although it helps that they can't actually acknowledge what was really stolen. The conspiracy nuts would have a field day with this, but Martin says that you saw a piece of the real Ark. How can you be so sure?"

Morgan was desperate to speak, to tell him of the overwhelming sense of awe she had felt in the presence of the sacred objects, of how she had wanted to fall down and worship whatever was causing the emotions to rise within her. She had felt the passion of David dancing before the

Ark, and she wanted to have that feeling again.

Was that what the mystics experienced when they saw God? Was that how her father felt when the sacred letters of the Torah danced before him as he studied Kabbalah? In the temple, she had glimpsed a glory she had only read about before, but how could she put that into words? And where was the Ark now? She tried to sit up.

"Try to relax," Marietti said. "Here, sip this."

He held a glass with a straw to her lips and Morgan sucked some of the cool water down. Her throat stung but she felt the lubrication begin to return.

"The Ark?" she whispered.

Marietti looked out of the window, staring off into the far distance as he spoke.

"That's the strange thing. We were expecting Natasha to take it to Jerusalem, to the Summit as the threats said, but she never showed up. We had security everywhere but it seems that she didn't even land in Jerusalem. She vanished along with the Ark pieces and we don't know why, or where she might have taken them." He looked at Morgan. "Which is why I need you to recover as fast as possible. You know more than anyone about how Natasha works, maybe you can find an insight that no one else can. Martin is still recovering, but he's working from his hospital bed and we're certainly suffering without him at HQ. I need you to think, Morgan, because we have to find that Ark. The immediate crisis has been averted, but the pieces can't be loose in the world for long, because too many groups would claim them as a powerful symbol. The Ark may not have sparked a war today, but it's still a flashpoint that could ignite violence at any point. In the wrong hands, it *will* bring war."

Morgan nodded. Her inner resolve hardened and this time there would be no room for error.

"The doctors say that you're lucky to have escaped with such minor injuries," Marietti said. "Your hand will take some time to heal properly, but you'll have full function back in the next few months. The smoke inhalation issues are minor complications and I know you've taken quite a beating, but can you hold out for a few more days?"

"Laptop?" Morgan wheezed out the word.

Marietti smiled at her unspoken assent.

"Of course, I'll have one brought over. You'll be able to access the ARKANE databases from here, but time is ticking Morgan. We must assume that the forces who employed Natasha are looking for her, as well as everyone else who knows about the Ark's existence. The Freemasons will be mobilizing a team and they have formidable forces available to them. I need you out of here in 48 hours, that's about as much time as we can spare."

Morgan mentally assessed the accumulated injuries in her body, the wheezing in her chest and her overall pain level. It was still below her threshold of giving up.

"I'll be out in four hours if you can get the drugs authorized," she whispered, looking at Marietti, her cobalt eyes metal-hard, the violet slash almost glowing. "Then I'll finish this."

Marietti nodded and stood up, turning to go. Then he wheeled back towards her.

"Morgan, I know there's vengeance in your heart - and rightly so - but search your conscience if you find Natasha. We now know that she's pregnant with Milan Noble's child so there is an innocent life at stake. If you find her, it will be up to you how you deal with her, but make the right decision, because the wrong one may haunt you for the rest of your life."

At that moment, Morgan glimpsed the secrets that this man kept, the souls that haunted his nights and the wrong decisions he had made. She saw her potential future and it was terrifying, then she blinked and the vision was lost.

CHAPTER 24

Hampstead, London. 11.32am

MORGAN WALKED DOWN THE leafy suburban street looking at blue plaques on the walls of the grand houses, marking the noted names of history who had once lived there. London was dotted with such markers, centuries of intellect layering the city in memory, and this area in particular was full of them.

In the last few hours, while the doctors patched her up and dosed her with drugs, Morgan had worked with Martin to delve further into Natasha's past, using ARKANE's access to secret records. Martin had even hacked into the database of the SSI, the Egyptian State Security Investigations Service, for information on several generations of El-Beherys. One thing had emerged with startling clarity.

They had found a reference to Natasha's grandfather, Daoud El-Behery, a contemporary of Sigmund Freud. He had been an educated businessman with global contacts, officially trading in antiquities, as well as a smuggler and an admirer of psychoanalysis. Freud had been a collector of antiquities and many of his artifacts had come from ancient Egypt, several pieces bearing the stamp of the El-Beherys that Daoud must have provided.

Morgan was convinced that Natasha would be hiding

somewhere that mattered to her emotionally, and perhaps these links to her family's past would shed some light on the theory. At this point, it was worth pursuing the hunch, because they had no other leads on where Natasha might be. It was a long shot, but perhaps Morgan would find some clue at the final resting place of Freud's Egyptian collection in London.

Sigmund Freud's old house at 20 Maresfield Gardens, Hampstead, was now a museum, so Morgan paid to enter like any other psychological tourist. Freud was always associated in her mind with Vienna, but when the Nazis came to power, Jews who could escape the worsening atmosphere left the city of waltzes, among them Freud and his family. They had arrived in England as refugees in 1938 when Freud was 82, and he had spent his final year in exile. London had become his refuge as Austria was torn apart by the Nazis, but Freud died at the outbreak of war, before the full scale of the atrocities against the Jews were displayed for all to see.

Morgan walked into Freud's study and looked around in wonder. It was the treasure cave of an eclectic mind, a psychological study in itself. The room was cramped, overflowing with myriad objects lining the shelves and erupting from corners. The walls were densely populated with books, all hardback and most leather bound. Morgan ran her fingers along the spines. The Tomb of Tutankhamun, Osiris: The Resurrection, The Golden Bough, Totemism and Exogamy. These were the books that Freud surrounded himself with, that soaked into his subconscious, that he saw when his mind wandered. They must have seeped into his thoughts, Morgan thought, and changed his world view.

Morgan found the Freud family Bible that had sparked his early interest in religion and the gods of Egypt, full of his underlinings in red, blue and green. She opened it to Deuteronomy Chapter 4 with its pictures of Egyptian gods with falcon heads, human faces and other idols. They referred to a text forbidding the worship of such creatures, but their very presence had ignited Freud's passion for ancient Egypt. The discussion of idolatry and polytheism was ironically what led Freud to return again and again to these figures.

On the shelves nearby were Egyptian mummy bandages inscribed with magical spells and stained with embalming ointment, superb Hellenistic statues and erotic Roman charms. The collection was an intriguing catalogue of world civilizations where objects rare and sacred, ravaged and lovely were on open display. Morgan thought about her own attic box, her secret treasures and saw that, in a similar way, this collection was Freud's mind made manifest. The things he had amassed were parts of him that he could externalize, representations of his personality. Perhaps her own house would be this full of history when she was in her eighties. If she made it that far, Morgan thought, as pain throbbed throughout her body.

She stood looking at Freud's desk, wondering about the man who had written here, the founder of what some would call the cult of psychoanalysis. The desk was sturdy wood, inset with red leather, a modest size given the huge shadow this man cast over psychology, European literature, art and science. There was only a small space for Freud to write, barely big enough for one A4 piece of paper, as about a third of the desk was taken up by two rows of figurines, gods who had sat watching him work.

Morgan bent to examine a marble baboon, a crescent moon on his head. This was one of the incarnations of the Egyptian god Thoth, the god of writing, knowledge and mysticism. The baboon was considered the most impulsive of the god's incarnations, the one connected to the instincts on which we all sometimes act. Perhaps it became the id of Freud's psychology, the base part that acts without thought, Morgan wondered. Yet Thoth was also the god who weighed the heart at the end of a life, according to the Book of the

Dead. If the heart weighed more than the feather of Ma'at, goddess of truth and justice, then the person would be cast into the jaws of Ammit, devourer of the dead.

Facing the desk on a low shelf were more busts of gods and Morgan wondered how Freud's writing practice worked? Perhaps they whispered divine truths to him, Morgan wondered, smiling at her whimsy. She examined Freud's chair, specially designed with a violin shaped back and thin but robust arms, for the psychologist had enjoyed sitting with one leg over the side of the chair when reading. It was reminiscent of a Henry Moore sculpture of a curvaceous woman, the mother figure inviting you to lie back in her arms.

On the floor, seemingly discarded, were two Egyptian stone funerary markers, hieroglyphics clearly marking the death of the King. Morgan smiled, for it was an amazing collection for an amateur. But then Freud had lived in the early 20th century when the great finds, Schliemann's Troy and Carter's Tutankhamun, were global news, and antiquity collecting was all the rage.

Morgan knew that Freud believed that the psychoanalyst was similar to an archaeologist, excavating layer after layer of the patient's psyche, before reaching the deepest and most precious treasures. Freud had a passion for uncovering secrets, for digging down and bringing the hidden to light, dusting off and piecing together the fragments of a shattered past.

Morgan turned slowly to take in the whole aspect. The study was a long double room with french windows hung with heavy curtains. The room had high ceilings and wooden floors but the space was dominated by the rich colors of Turkish rugs and carpets. The deep reds and golds made the room feel cozier somehow, more like a secret chamber.

Moving to the other end of the study, Morgan noticed a Rembrandt print of Moses holding the Tablets of the Law which had been stored in the Ark of the Covenant. It was a black and white cross-hatched drawing with Hebrew letters dominating the scene. She knew that the figure of Moses had haunted Freud for much of his life.

While visiting Rome, he had become intrigued by Michelangelo's statue of Moses at St Peter in Vinculi. The statue was horned, due to a mistranslation of the Hebrew for shining, but the horns somehow gave the figure a gravitas, and Freud had studied and sketched it for weeks. It showed the moment when Moses came down from the mountain with the tablets of the Ten Commandments and found the Israelites worshipping false gods. His anger was such that he smashed the tablets of God in two.

Morgan had read Freud's last book, 'Moses and Monotheism'. In it he had suggested that Moses had been an Egyptian and a priest in the Aten monotheistic cult, a member of the royal house of Akhenaten. When Akhenaten died, and the cult abolished, Moses found new advocates in the Hebrews, at that time a slave group working on the cities and monuments of Egypt. Moses organized the Hebrews and became their leader, making Egyptian monotheism the basis of their religion. After the Exodus from Egypt, Freud postulated that the Egyptian Jews overthrew and killed Moses, his murder becoming a repressed memory that echoed through their violent history.

Turning from the Moses image, Morgan noticed a print of Abu Simbel, the gigantic temple built in southern Egypt, standing at the edge of the desert to intimidate barbarian hordes. Three giant heads of Pharaoh Rameses II looked out over the waters of the River Nile, a starry sky above them lighting the faces of the ancient kings. A fourth figure crumbled near the central entrance to the tomb from which a light shone as if the temple were in use again, a resurrection of long-dead faith in the modern world.

There was an inscription on the print. Morgan leaned closer to read it and gasped, for it had been gifted to Freud by

Daoud El-Behery, Natasha's grandfather. Had he had shared his love and dreams of the place with his granddaughter? Looking at the light in the Temple, Morgan wondered if perhaps that dream was being lived out right now.

CHAPTER 25

Abu Simbel, Southern Egypt. 11.23pm

IT WAS PITCH BLACK as the tiny plane banked towards the location of Abu Simbel, in the great red desert 230km south west of Aswan, the nearest city. Morgan looked out of the window into the night, wondering if she had just made a terrible mistake in bringing the team here. This was the only lead she had and if she didn't find Natasha now, others could find the Ark first.

"The pilot says he'll be able to land using instruments only," Nejev, one of the ARKANE local team, said from his seat further forward. Morgan nodded. She had wanted to come alone but Marietti had insisted on a small group to accompany her, given Natasha's tendency for violence. "But it looks pretty desolate out there," Nejev continued. "How do you want to proceed on landing?"

"We'll proceed to the Temple with caution," Morgan said, "but if she's here, I think she'll be inside at the main altar."

"A couple of men will stay with the plane and I'll bring two men along with me as your escort."

Nejev seemed professional and courteous, but Morgan's thoughts returned to Jake and the night assault they had undertaken together in Tunisia during the hunt for the Pentecost stones. She missed her partner.

The plane bumped down on the deserted airstrip and came to a halt near the entrance building. There was a wire fence but the area was so far away from any cities that there was no need for any enhanced security measures. By day, charter flights brought tourist groups here to marvel, but by night, the ruins were deserted.

Morgan moved to the front of the plane as Nejev briefed his men. She started to open the door.

"Wait, stop!" one of the men shouted from the back. "Don't open the door. I'm reading heat signatures around the edge of the airstrip."

Morgan turned, her eyes alive now, the violet slash bright. "She's here. We have to get to the Temple. Is there anywhere I could slip through?"

The man tapped on his laptop.

"It looks like they have a less protected area, south west from here. You could slip past there."

Morgan turned to Nejev. "You need to cover my route to the edge of the fence. I'll take one other man with me but we need to be quick and silent. If you can keep the forces occupied we may be able to make the Temple un-noticed."

"If you go out the maintenance hatch under the plane, we'll open the door at the same time and create a diversion for you. If we can hold them here, thinking we're pinned inside, you should have enough time to get through. We'll let you know any changes in position through the headset."

Grabbing her backpack and pulling on the communications device, Morgan motioned for one of the men to follow her. Together they ducked down into the maintenance hatch and out underneath the plane. It was still pitch black and slowly Morgan's eyes adapted to the dark.

The air was close and warm and a bead of sweat trickled down her back as she stood silently, listening to the night. It was still, with only the slight noises of desert animals scurrying through the dust of the dead kingdom, preda-tors that hunted here on the edge of scarcity. But she knew that Natasha's men were out there, silently waiting for the moment when the occupants of the plane emerged.

Then she heard the front and rear doors of the plane open, both on the west side. A low voice came through the microphone in her ear.

"The heat signatures show the men moving around to encircle the open doors. You should be able to run east and circle back to the fence line." Morgan nodded at the man with her. He nodded back in readiness. Then the gunfire started.

Trusting Nejev to handle the combat situation, Morgan ran low and fast away from the plane towards the fence. A few meters from the fence, a burst of gunfire came from the trees in front of them. The man with her dropped to the ground, grunting in pain. Pulling her Sig Sauer P229, Morgan fired back towards the shadowy figure as she ran zigzagging towards the fence. The figure fell and the gunfire stopped. But there would be more men, she only had a small window of opportunity now.

"Man down," she whispered into the microphone. "He's on the tarmac, still alive."

"We'll send someone out to bring him back in," Nejev's voice came over the comms device. "But wait, Morgan, I'll send another man out to you."

"No time," she whispered back. "I'm going in alone."

Using the wire cutters from her pack, Morgan made a hole and squeezed through it, using her pack to protect her body against the barbs. On the other side, she pushed her way through the dense trees and bushes, guided by the tall cliff she could see looming above her. The sound of gunfire receded as she moved quickly and quietly away from the airstrip. But she reloaded the Sig anyway and held it ready as she proceeded. She wouldn't underestimate Natasha again.

A few minutes later, Morgan rounded a corner in the

path and emerged at the feet of Pharaoh Ramses II, his body rising twenty meters above her. There were four such statues, colossal kings carved in the rock, all wearing the double Atef crown of Upper and Lower Egypt. Statues of his family stood life-size by his feet and a frieze of twenty-two baboons danced across the top of the temple, alive in a petrified jungle of ancient adoration. The temple was designed for the worship of the Pharaoh but also the state deities of Egypt, Ra-Harakhty, Ptah and Amun. Next to the main temple was another smaller one where Nefertari, his queen, was venerated as the goddess Hathor.

Morgan knew that the gigantic temples were originally carved into the rock faces of a huge escarpment in Nubia, southern Egypt. They faced the tribes coming out of black sub-Saharan Africa, the gaze of the mammoth pharaohs an intimidation and a warning of the might of Egypt. The temples had been moved during the building of Lake Nasser when the Nile had been dammed and a huge Lake drowned everything behind it. To save the temples, they had been dismantled, cut into huge blocks and rebuilt high above the old location. Lake Nasser had been called the scourge of Egypt, altering the ancient rhythms of the Nile flooding that had refreshed the country for millennia, for the dam had flooded the heartland of the Nubian people, making them refugees in their own country.

Morgan looked away from the temple towards the lake, as the cry of a night bird broke the silence. It was quiet, too quiet, she thought, but perhaps that meant all the men were up at the airstrip. She proceeded with caution but the only way into the Temple was the entrance that stretched out between the feet of the mammoth statues. There was no other way in, so she crept out across the vista of the temple, a shadow silhouetted by the spotlights, acutely aware that she could be seen by anyone watching.

Between the great pharaohs, a corridor led into the main

temple, a dark maw in the cliffs. There was nowhere to hide, no vegetation, no statues, just an open corridor to the inner sanctum and she couldn't see inside. Then she heard the faintest sound of singing, a hymn to the gods. Morgan pulled her gun and moved forward, keeping it trained on the dark hole in front of her.

A sharp noise came from behind. Morgan turned and a powerful blow exploded on her jaw, spinning her round, her gun and communications device knocked into the sand. She reeled back, away from the figure of Natasha's bodyguard, Isac.

"Now we will finish what my mistress started in London," he said. "This is a fitting place for the sacrifice of such a warrior, for you will die at my hands."

Morgan saw the glimmer in his eye as he spoke of Natasha and she saw a defense in goading him.

"Why are you here, Isac? Why didn't she take the pieces of the Ark to Jerusalem?" He lunged at her, and Morgan jumped back, aware of the damage his fists could do to her already bruised body. "You know the baby isn't yours, don't you?"

His eyes flashed and she realized that he hadn't known for sure about the child Natasha carried. He ran at her, enraged. Morgan stood her ground and then twisted at the last moment, grabbing his arm and bending it back on itself. In one movement, she stomped on the back of his knee and Isac went down, but he didn't seem aware of the pain and exploded up at her, the back of his head missing her face by millimeters. She let him go and ran, diving for her gun in the sand, but he caught her ankle, pulling her down with a thump. Morgan groaned as her battered body reeled at the shot of pain, but she clawed forwards, kicking sand in his face, even as he pulled his way up her body.

"You will pay," he roared, and she heard all the anger he had been repressing, the desire to protect Natasha even though he could never possess her. Morgan's fingertips touched the gun, but Isac reached up and pulled her hand down so it slipped from her grasp.

As her fingers raked through the sand, they touched a rock. She grabbed it and used all her strength to roll, bringing the rock hard down onto Isac's face, smashing into his eye socket. He howled and clutched at it with one hand while he pulled at her with the other, but it was enough of a distraction. Morgan crawled to her gun, spun and fired it as Isac launched himself at her. His momentum carried him forward on top of her, but the surprise in his eyes was complete as he coughed up blood and Morgan pulled herself out from under him. Isac reached out towards the temple.

"Natasha," he whispered as his eyes glazed over and he joined the pharaohs in the Underworld. Morgan knelt briefly to close his eyes for she understood the value of loyalty and hoped someone would do the same for her one day.

She stood and cautiously approached the temple entrance again. The men from the plane would have heard the gunshot so they would be on their way, but she wanted to meet Natasha on her own, so she entered quietly.

As her eyes adjusted to the dark, she could make out tall pillars within and as she crept inside, she saw that they were carved with seated Ramses dressed as the risen Osiris. Bas-reliefs of battle scenes lined the walls. Morgan knew that the axis of the temple was such that twice a year on the solstices, rays of sun would penetrate the sanctuary and illuminate the statues on the back wall. The gods would see the sun, except for Ptah, God of the Underworld, who always remained in the dark.

The eerie singing weaved its way around the columns of the temple, mingling with the whistle of the wind through the ancient stone. Morgan walked slowly further into the temple, finally reaching the main chamber where Natasha knelt in front of an altar upon which lay the wrapped pieces of the Ark. A brazier stood on each side of the altar, a cloying, sweet smoke hazy in the air. Between bursts of song, Natasha drank deep from a copper bowl, gulping the contents down.

Morgan stepped out into the corridor, gun in front of her, and remembered Marietti's words. How she dealt with Natasha was her decision, but it would also be on her conscience. Now she knew for sure about the baby, she couldn't just shoot the woman, for it was no longer just one life at stake. Morgan suddenly found that the rage and need for revenge that had driven her until now had blown away like ash from a funeral pyre, leaving only a bitter taste in her mouth. What drove her now was the need to protect Israel from the threat of destruction and the Ark could only ever be a danger to her beloved country.

"It's over, Natasha," Morgan said, her voice absorbing into the walls that had borne witness to so many prayers across millennia.

The singing stopped and Natasha laughed without turning.

"Why am I not surprised you found me, Morgan? I thought at least the men would contain you at the airstrip until I had finished. But it's too late now anyway." She stood and turned, pulling back her cloak to reveal a suicide bomber's vest. "Now you will die here with me."

Morgan could see that it wasn't armed yet. There was still time, but clearly Natasha had no desire to leave this place alive and she was on the edge of some kind of mania.

"Why didn't you take the Ark to Jerusalem?" Morgan asked.

Natasha was defiant, her piercing eyes gleaming with recognition of a truth that went beyond mortal understanding.

"You know why," she said, "because you felt it too. In London, you felt the power of the Ark touch you deep inside, didn't you? So you must understand. It wouldn't let me take it to Jerusalem, for the Ark can only be restored there in the end times and they are not at hand. I didn't believe it before, but now I know."

Morgan could hear fanaticism in her voice, but she remembered the brief touch of the Ark in the Grand Temple and how she had felt in its presence. Natasha was a faithful servant of the ancient Egyptian gods and yet she was obeying the power of the Jewish Ark, so there was clearly something powerful here.

Natasha walked to the altar and began to unwrap a piece of the Ark, peeling the covering off it with her bare hands.

"Don't do it," Morgan pleaded, her gun wavering as her hands shook. Part of her was desperate to know what might happen and yet the biblical verses about the deadly power of the Ark made her want to stop what might happen.

Natasha's laugh rang out as she continued to pull the coverings back, revealing each piece, twelve in all, gathered from the Masonic lodges across England, plus the piece from Ethiopia.

"Perhaps nothing will happen," she said. "Perhaps there is no power in the Ark, perhaps there never was. It is a talisman of a dead world and it's fitting that it should die here, in this place of death." Her voice became wistful. "And I will stay with it, watching over the lake and looking north towards my Egypt."

As she unwrapped the last piece of the Ark, Morgan saw that they were beginning to glow, and the sound of rushing waters filled the cavernous hall. Freckles of gold on the wood became translucent and shining, like a mirror reflecting the sun with shimmers of a place beyond. Morgan blinked, trying to clear her vision from what must be some kind of hallucination, or perhaps the smoke was affecting her perception. Natasha's eyes were wide with excitement and wonder.

"The Ark is alive again," she said with delight, placing both her hands on the altar. "I can feel its energy building."

Morgan wanted to step closer, to touch it herself, but she knew from the Bible that this was an ancient weapon, a way in which the Israelites had killed other tribes. This energy had torn down the thick stone walls of Jericho. What could it do to this place?

A deep throbbing began to oscillate from the altar. Natasha threw back her head and called out a prayer to her own gods as light seemed to pulse from within her, channeled through the fragments of the Ark. Morgan backed away down the corridor as the smoke from the braziers swirled up as if moved by a whirlwind.

A shaft of light broke from the Ark, piercing the darkness, and there was a hissing sound where the ray struck the wall. Morgan could see the stone smoking as it was dissolved, like acid on skin. Another ray lanced out and struck a column which began to hiss in the same way.

Morgan slid behind one of the stone pillars. She wanted to run, but something held her to the spot as a witness. Was this a manifestation of the Ark or was she hallucinating from drug-laden smoke? A ray shot straight down from the altar into the earth and a crack opened up, then another slanted into the ceiling and a chunk of stone dropped down, smashing into the floor.

Natasha was standing transfixed by the light, a conduit for the energy flowing through her, calling in triumph to the gods. Suddenly, a ray shot out and pierced her through, lifting her into the air. She was held suspended, writhing on the beam. Morgan saw desperate horror on her face, as if she was faced with the very demons of hell, and then the light on the suicide vest turned green as it was armed by her jerking movements.

Morgan turned and ran as the shafts of light seemed to explode through the floor behind her, burning the path down which she ran. She made it into the tunnel between the great statues of Pharaoh and then the explosion lifted her off her feet, catapulting her away from the temple onto the burning sand by the lake. Missiles of ancient rock rained down around her as she held her arms up to protect her head.

The initial explosion was followed by a deep boom, sounding from well below the earth. The ground shook and it seemed as if a pillar of fire and smoke whirled above the temple. The statues of Pharaoh crumbled, the great head-dresses falling apart and Morgan pulled herself up and ran again, hobbling to the water's edge, as far from the temple as she could get. She found that she was sobbing, as if she was witnessing the very end of the world.

THE DAY AFTER

CHAPTER 26

Oxford, England. 6.15pm

MORGAN WATCHED AS JAKE'S chest rose and fell smoothly as he breathed. The hospital room was much quieter than before, as most of the monitoring instruments were gone now Jake had recovered enough to be revived from the artificial coma. Martin had already been in and Morgan was desperate to wake Jake and talk, but that was just selfish. He needed rest, not her angst. Jake lay on his back, and although his face was thinner, he no longer looked like a corpse. She sat on the chair by his bed, closing her eyes, grateful for the peace and quiet.

It had been a long day of debriefing in London, because the destruction of Abu Simbel meant that ARKANE had had to come up with a convincing story. Morgan had sat in Director Marietti's office sipping thick, black coffee all day as they had worked through the press statements. Finally, the media had been told that the responsibility for the bombing had been claimed by an Islamic extremist group who believed that the temples were idols in the Muslim country and must be destroyed. It was plausible enough, given the evidence of the gunfight, and there was still a great deal of international attention focused on conflict in Israel, so the furore would die down soon enough.

"Hey there." Jake's voice was croaky and hoarse.

Morgan opened her eyes, smiling at him.

"Hey yourself." She reached for his hand and squeezed it, overwhelmed with relief that he was going to be fine. Jake returned the pressure as their eyes communicated what they would never say out loud to each other.

"I heard you blew up a UNESCO World Heritage site," Jake said, his grin as cheeky as ever. Morgan shook her head in mock despair.

"And I did some serious damage to the Temple of the United Grand Lodge of England," she giggled. "ARKANE has a lot of clearing up to do, but Marietti's being pretty good about it."

"Sounds like you need a partner to keep you out of trouble," Jake said.

"Sure, great help you would have been. You couldn't even stay conscious."

Jake laughed, then grimaced and coughed violently, his body jerking. Morgan watched anxiously as he recovered his breath.

"I'll be back with you soon, I promise." His voice seemed a lot stronger than his body and Morgan leaned in close.

"Don't tell Marietti," she whispered, "but to be honest, I could use a rest. I've been shot at, beaten, stabbed, burned and blown up this week." She paused. "And I find myself conflicted about what really happened."

Jake nodded. "Martin told me about the search for the Ark and I'm pissed to have missed out on all the fun. Did they find it in the wreckage?"

Morgan shook her head. "There was nothing left in the ruins of the sanctuary. No human remains, no pieces of the Ark, not even an altar. There's nothing to explain the blast or to back up my explanation of events."

"Morgan, I believe you, so does Marietti. This is ARKANE, this is what we do. I see the haunted look in your eyes and

I know of the lore of the Ark. But the pieces weren't meant to be together again. It wasn't time and perhaps Natasha did the right thing in the end."

Morgan shook her head.

"I just keep coming up against things I can't explain. It's frustrating because I wanted to study those pieces of the Ark, to understand how that kind of energy could work. But I wanted to do it in a lab, away from hallucinogenic smoke and an atmosphere of superstition. Now I can't ever know what was real or why I felt the way I did."

Jake squeezed her hand.

"Let it go, Morgan. There are mysteries that we can never solve, that we can only grasp at. ARKANE exists to keep the balance, to make sure that these mysteries don't emerge and disrupt a world that isn't ready for them. We won this time, albeit through a strange route, but there will be another battle tomorrow, and next time I'll face it with you."

* * *

Morgan's adventures continue in
One Day in Budapest, available now.

A relic, stolen from the heart of an ancient city.
An echo of nationalist violence not seen since the
dark days of the Second World War.

Budapest, Hungary. When a priest is murdered at the Basilica of St Stephen and the Holy Right relic is stolen, the ultra-nationalist Eröszak party calls for retribution and anti-Semitic violence erupts in the city.

Dr Morgan Sierra, psychologist and ARKANE agent, finds herself trapped inside the synagogue with Zoltan Fischer, a Hungarian Jewish security advisor. As the terrorism escalates, Morgan and Zoltan must race against time to find the Holy Right and expose the conspiracy, before blood is spilled again on the streets of Budapest.

ENJOYED ARK OF BLOOD?

If you loved the book and have a moment to spare, I would really appreciate a short review on the page where you bought the book. Your help in spreading the word is gratefully appreciated and reviews make a huge difference to helping new readers find the series. Thank you!

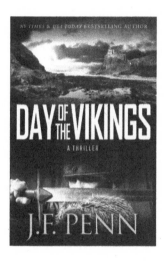

Get a free copy of the bestselling thriller, *Day of the Vikings*, ARKANE book 5, when you sign up to join my Reader's Group. You'll also be notified of new releases, giveaways and receive personal updates from behind the scenes of my thrillers.

WWW.JFPENN.COM/FREE

Day of the Vikings, an ARKANE thriller

A ritual murder on a remote island under the shifting skies of the aurora borealis.

A staff of power that can summon Ragnarok, the Viking apocalypse.

When Neo-Viking terrorists invade the British Museum in London to reclaim the staff of Skara Brae, ARKANE agent Dr. Morgan Sierra is trapped in the building along with hostages under mortal threat.

As the slaughter begins, Morgan works alongside psychic Blake Daniel to discern the past of the staff, dating back to islands invaded by the Vikings generations ago.

Can Morgan and Blake uncover the truth before Ragnarok is unleashed, consuming all in its wake?

Day of the Vikings is a fast-paced, supernatural thriller set in London and the islands of Orkney, Lindisfarne and Iona. Set in the present day, it resonates with the history and myth of the Vikings.

If you love an action-packed thriller,
you can get Day of the Vikings for free now:

WWW.JFPENN.COM/FREE

Day of the Vikings features Dr. Morgan Sierra from the ARKANE thrillers, and Blake Daniel from the London Crime Thrillers, but it is also a stand-alone novella that can be read and enjoyed separately.

AUTHOR'S NOTE

With my ARKANE thrillers, I want to keep as much anchored in the truth as possible but then extend it into the fictional realm to give you a story that is (almost) believable.

Research is my addiction, and with this book, I was keen to investigate the awesome history and speculation about the Ark of the Covenant, as well as tie it to political events that could erupt at any moment in the Middle East. Here are some of the interesting facts behind the fiction. As ever, any mistakes are my own.

You can find detailed hyperlinks here:
www.jfpenn.com/exodus-research

Israel, the Falasha and Middle Eastern politics

* In 2011, non-Muslims were banned from the Temple Mount and the ban is still in force as of November 2012 because of the threat of violence.

* Extreme right wing Jewish groups exist who aim to build the Third Temple on the site, for example, the Temple Mount Faithful.

* The Falasha, also called Beta-Israel, are a group of Ethiopian Jews who were given right of return in 1977. There

are around 100,000 in Israel but it is reported that they are treated like second-class citizens and experience racism. As a minority group they have little political power. One article reports their desperate plight, with at least 30 cases of depressed and unemployed Falasha men killing their families and then themselves in murder-suicides. One man says, *"Not a day goes by without someone treating me like a cockroach because of the color of my skin."*

I wanted to have a 'home-grown' terrorist in Avi Kabede, and using the plight of the Falasha as a motive has at least some ring of truth to it.

* Yasser Arafat's body has recently been exhumed to check for polonium poisoning (November 2012)

Moses and Akhenaten

That Moses was an Egyptian seems to be well established by the academic sources, and the research on the early monotheism of Akhenaten certainly fits with the story of Exodus and also the design of the Ark. Here's some further reading:

* Moses and Akhenaten: The secret history of Egypt at the time of the Exodus - Ahmed Osman

* Myths and legends of ancient Egypt - Joyce Tyldesley

The possible locations of the Ark of the Covenant

For an overview of the rumored locations of the Ark, you can read the Wikipedia article. For more detail, here are some of the books I read and recommend:

* The Lost Ark of the Covenant - Tudor Parfitt. This fantastic book covers the journey of the author into Africa to investigate the Lemba and also Aksum in Ethiopia.

* The Quest for the Ark of the Covenant - Stuart Munro-Hay

* Lost Secrets of the Sacred Ark by Laurence Gardner. The science of mono-atomic gold, high-spin, super-conductors and quantum physics is definitely beyond me so I include a mere mention of it here.

Codex Sinaiticus

The fragments were controversially removed from the Monastery of St Catherine and are now kept in the British Library in London, with some pieces at other museums. You can read more and watch a video here: www.jfpenn.com/codex-sinaiticus-palimpsest

John Soane Museum

The John Soane Museum in London is a treasure trove of classical sculpture and all kinds of strange objects, including the sarcophagus of Seti I. Soane did build an Ark of the Masonic Covenant for the Grand Lodge, and it (supposedly) burned down in the fire of 1863.

Sir Charles Warren and the Palestine Exploration Fund

Both Charles Warren and the PEF were real but I invented the side trip to Jordan in the unofficial records as well as embellishing the way in which Warren got the top job of Police Commissioner.

Freemasonry

The United Grand Lodge of England in London is a real place and you can visit, as I did one cloudy afternoon. The description of the Lodge is mostly true, but I didn't enter the room on the left of the altar. The coat of arms does have the Ark of the Covenant on it but they don't (officially) claim to have it.

The George Washington Masonic Memorial, Washington DC, is also a real place and I was stunned to find that they have a replica Ark, complete with a mural of the destroyed Temple on the wall.

Freud Museum, Hampstead

The descriptions of Freud's office and antiquities collection at the house, now a museum, is all written from a visit I made. You can read more and see some photos here: www. joannapenn.com/freud-museum/

* Moses and Monotheism - Sigmund Freud. The theories on Moses as an Egyptian, his murder in the desert of Sinai and the collective guilt for this act

* Freud and Moses: the long journey home - Emanuel Rice. Freud called himself 'the godless Jew,' but did he return to his faith in his final book?

Abu Simbel

I travelled to Abu Simbel on a trip around Egypt, and I always wanted it to be the location of the climactic scene for this book. When I found a painting of it on Sigmund Freud's wall, I knew his obsession with Egypt and Moses would add another dimension to the story. More information and pictures here: www.jfpenn.com/abu-simbel

MORE BOOKS BY J.F.PENN

Thanks for joining Morgan, Jake and the
ARKANE team. The adventures continue …

Stone of Fire #1
Crypt of Bone #2
Ark of Blood #3
One Day in Budapest #4
Day of the Vikings #5
Gates of Hell #6
One Day in New York #7
Destroyer of Worlds #8
End of Days #9
Valley of Dry Bones #10

If you like **crime thrillers with an edge of the supernatural**,
join Detective Jamie Brooke and museum researcher Blake
Daniel, in the London Crime Thriller trilogy:

Desecration #1
Delirium #2
Deviance #3

If you enjoy **dark fantasy,** check out:

Map of Shadows, Mapwalkers #1
Risen Gods
American Demon Hunters: Sacrifice

A Thousand Fiendish Angels:
Short stories based on Dante's Inferno

The Dark Queen

More books coming soon.

You can sign up to be notified of new releases, giveaways
and pre-release specials - plus, get a free book!

WWW.JFPENN.COM/FREE

ABOUT J.F.PENN

J.F.Penn is the Award-nominated, New York Times and USA Today bestselling author of the ARKANE supernatural thrillers, London Crime Thrillers, and the Mapwalker dark fantasy series, as well as other standalone stories.

Her books weave together ancient artifacts, relics of power, international locations and adventure with an edge of the supernatural. Joanna lives in Bath, England and enjoys a nice G&T.

* * *

You can sign up for a free thriller,
Day of the Vikings, and updates from behind the scenes,
research, and giveaways at:

WWW.JFPENN.COM/FREE

* * *

Connect at:
www.JFPenn.com
joanna@JFPenn.com
www.Facebook.com/JFPennAuthor
www.Instagram.com/JFPennAuthor
www.Twitter.com/JFPennWriter

* * *

For writers:

Joanna's site, www.TheCreativePenn.com, helps people write, publish and market their books through articles, audio, video and online courses.

She writes non-fiction for authors under Joanna Penn and has an award-nominated podcast for writers, The Creative Penn Podcast.

ACKNOWLEDGEMENTS

AS ALWAYS, MY LOVE and thanks to Jonathan, best husband and my first reader.

Thanks to my line editor, Jacqueline Penn (my Mum!) who continues to improve my writing through challenging my word choices and spotting my repetitions. Thanks also to my cover designer, Derek Murphy who did another fantastic job: www.bookcovers.creativindie.com and to Liz Broomfield from www.LibroEditing.com for proof-reading the final draft. Thanks to JD Smith Design www.jdsmith-design.co.uk for the interior formatting on the print version.

A huge thank you to my beta-readers: my friend and-mentor Orna Ross www.OrnaRoss.com who encourages me to go deeper into my themes; action-adventure author David Wood www.davidwoodonline.blogspot.com who always picks up on fight scene issues; and to Arthur Penn, my Dad who is also an art history specialist and writer himself. I couldn't have done it without you guys.

The biggest thank you goes out to my readers. I hope to keep delighting you with new books!

Printed in June 2019
by Rotomail Italia S.p.A., Vignate (MI) - Italy